Elphie Earns Her Wings

Courage, Empathy, and Teamwork

by S. C. Delaney

Elphie Earns Her Wings

Copyright © 2024 by S. C. Delaney

RHG Media Productions
21519 Knoll Way,
Castro Valley, CA 94546.

ISBN 979-8-9902463-0-0 (paperback)
ISBN 979-8-9902463-1-7 (hardcover)

Visit us on line at www.YourPurposeDrivenPractice.com
Printed in the United States of America.

What People Are Saying

"A delightful narrative that will inspire and uplift children and people of all ages."
    —**Finn O'Malley, bestselling author of the** *Keeper of Elements* **series and GLOWup series**

"Elphie Earns Her Wings is a whimsical tale celebrating spiritedness, teamwork, and inclusion . . . Delaney gracefully balances a poignant parent-child story with imaginative world-building. Readers-both young and young at heart-will cherish Elphie's ability to promote courage and celebrate uniqueness."
    —**Fallyn Adams, 5/6 math and science teacher, Rockland, ME**

"When it comes to perseverance, spirit, and courageous fun, no one tops the fixie Elphie. Readers of any age will discover that your differences can be your ultimate strengths and that love (especially for yourself), can create beautiful magic."
    —**Hannah R. Lyon, bestselling fantasy author and comprehensive editor**

"A delightful fable that, through expressively colorful imagery, paints a fantastical world where all of creation is (literally) alive."
    —**Dr. Nancy Tarr Hart, PhD, author,** *Beyond the Veil: Unmasking the Feminine* **(Volume 1); and,** *Unraveling the Mystery of Mary* **(Volume 2)**

"S.C. Delaney creates a believable fantasy world and crafts a tale of friendship, teamwork, and self-discovery that is charming, entrancing, and inspiring."
    —**Carl Weaver, president, Broken Column Press; author,** *Next Life in the Afternoon: A Journey Through Thailand*

"I couldn't put it down . . . Elphie's story illustrates to the young and the young at heart that there is no one else who can be YOU, and that's a good thing! Wonderful, simply wonderful!! I can't wait to see what the future holds for Elphie and S.C. Delaney."

—JoAnn Harris, cofounder of A Hand Up, Huntsville, AL

"Through Elphie's experiences, the author demonstrates that love transcends differences and is a powerful force to bring individuals and communities together."

—Tina Kay, author and cohost on Dare to Rise podcast

"Elphie Earns Her Wings by S.C. Delaney is a delightfully whimsical adventure of bravery and friendship. Through kindness, teamwork, and belief in others, this little fixie learns it's okay to be different and that love is truly the universal language."

—Tiffani Freckleton RN, bestselling author of *My NICU Story: Written with Love* and coauthor of the *Award-Winning Letters to a Future Nurse*

"I could not put this book down, as the world that S.C. Delaney created had me captivated from start to finish."

—Misti Mazurik, Director of Operations, RHG Media Productions

"It's a delightful story you will read more than once."

—Elda Robinson, international bestselling author of *One More Thing*

"Our community heavily shapes who we become. This is especially true for Elphie Askul."

—Cherese A. Vines, author of *Countercharm*

"The life lessons in every turn of the page keeps Elphie alive and makes you want to keep turning the page to see how she survives what's next in her path to overcome, turning those obstacles into lessons of growth for all involved."

—Steve Zeiger, international bestselling author of *My Lights: The True Story of an Authentic Life*

Dedication

To my beautiful Wife, my amazing Mum, and my
wonderful Mother-In-Law, and all the strong women
I have been blessed to have in my life.

Table of Contents

Cast of Characters

CHARACTER	IDENTITY
Marri Golde	Fairy, Elphie's mother
Po	Pixie, Elphie's father
Nahke	Oak tree, Marri Golde and Po's Home Tree
Wonderfolke	Eludian name for fairies and pixies
Elphie Askul	Fixie, daughter of Marri Golde and Po
Ryart	Hedgehog, Elphie's friend
Jewels	Flying squirrel, Elphie's friend
Condor, Crow Kueen	Crow leader, enemy of fairies and pixies
Alice	Titan beetle, friend of fairies and pixies
Zima, Willder Bees' Queen	Honeybee leader, friend of fairies and pixies
Willder Bees	Honeybee, friends of fairies and pixies
Mortimer	Bear, enemy of the Willder bees
Bulli	Badger, inhabitant of Freedo's Pond
Honus	Hoo bird, inhabitant of Southern Forest
Monarch Queen	Monarch butterfly leader, inhabitant of Milkweed Fields

Introduction

O nce upon a dewdrop, pixies and fairies lived together in the land of Eludia.

Moon and Sun populated their secret land with their favorite living things, allowing the animals they chose to live their lives, have children, and then eventually transition from this world to the next.

It's unclear whether a fairy or pixie first discovered Eludia (the old knowledge is lost), but what is known is that the powers of both fairies and pixies were needed to create their home in Eludia. Here they lived separately, but together, in a cluster of home trees called Homestead. Moon and Sun allowed their presence, but they dictated that fairies and pixies could never blend their families.

The Wonderfolke obliged. Those who transgressed were banished from Homestead.

Po and Marri Golde were one such couple that was exiled. The pixie and fairy were deeply in love. This is the story of their daughter, Elphie Askul.

Marri Golde and Po

"We must go." Po pulled his wife close. He was large for a pixie, nearly as tall as a sunflower head with thighs like a grasshopper. Marri Golde was a full inchworm shorter, but average height for a fairy. Her arms and legs were like wisps of grass and her torso was the width of a sunflower stalk. The only similarity between the fairy and pixie was their wings—each pair was a shimmering translucence. They should never have fallen in love. It was forbidden by the Moon and Sun above.

Fairies and pixies were not supposed to interwed, but Po loved his wife like the rising moon, and Marri Golde loved her husband like the morning sun. Because he was a pixie and she was a fairy, the two had been banished from Homestead by the Grand Troupe Council over four hundred years ago for the simple act of being in love.

Together, Marri Golde and Po created their own troupe, and lived alone on the outskirts of their community, southeast of Homestead. In all of Eludia, their love was only understood by Po and Marri Golde's troupe.

A pixie or fairy's family unit was called a troupe. The troupe a fairy or pixie was born into was their familial troupe (the family you grew up with). The Grand Troupe was made up of all the familial troupes. All familial troupes were governed by the Grand Troupe Council, which was composed of elected representatives from all the fairy and pixie troupes.

Marri Golde and Po's troupe included the two of them and their home tree, Nahke. Their troupe was different than other troupes, but not because of the inclusion of their home tree; Nahke understood their love. It was unusual because Marri Golde was a fairy and Po was a pixie. Familial troupes were never mixed.

But Po and Marri Golde thought that rule did not make sense because their love made sense to them. It was real. Palpable. The Grand Troupe consisted of all the familial troupes in Eludia, and that included fairy troupes and pixie troupes. Fairies and pixies were mixed at the highest levels of leadership; why not with a familial troupe?

"And," fumed Po one autumn eve, "familial troupes include home trees, so why couldn't a familial troupe have other non-fairies or non-pixies? Because it makes no sense, is why."

Po and Marri Golde's home tree, Nahke, was a sturdy oak tree who sat on a hill overlooking the warm, pink milkweed fields. The fairy and pixie first bonded with their home tree nearly four hundred years ago, shortly after being banished around the age of two hundred. Prior to their banishment, Marri Golde and Po had been going to Milkweed Fields once a year for their entire lives to witness the Emergence. Everyone in Homestead traveled for the ceremony.

The Emergence was one of the core rituals of fairies and pixies. Other ceremonies were performed when a new familial troupe was created: a tree became a Home Tree; or the birth of a child; or the transition of a fairy or pixie from this world to the next. The Emergence was important because that's when the spent chrysalises of the monarch butterflies were harvested by the pixies. The chrysalises were essential to the way of life of all fairies and pixies. One Emergence provided enough material to clothe the greater community of Homestead for a year. In addition, it was used to make bags, rugs, mattresses, cushions, and other necessaries.

The ceremony was different from the other rituals because it was a communal activity attended by nearly everyone in the Grand Troupe. Most ceremonies were only attended by members of one's familial troupe.

The Emergence was held the day the monarch butterflies emerged from the milkweed fields. The fields were outside of Homestead, and the Grand Troupe traveled together to the event. The pixies worked the fields while the Luna troupe's youngest adult female led the ritual. When Marri Golde turned one hundred, it became her turn to lead the ceremony.

The first butterfly to leave a cocoon was named the "Monarch Queen" by the Grand Troupe Council. The Emergence was the queen's coronation.

During the ritual, the lead fairy bestowed the gift of life to the Monarch Queen. Where most butterflies live for just over a moon cycle, the Monarch Queen was given a sliver of wing from the fairy leading the ceremony. The queen's consumption of this gift allowed the butterfly to live ten times longer than any other butterfly. Her reign began with her emergence and extended for the duration of the butterflies' migration from Milkweed Fields to the four corners of Eludia. Her reign ended upon her return and the laying of her eggs in the same milkweed field she had first emerged from, nearly a year before.

Butterflies do not normally have a queen, but the fairies and pixies installed the tradition. By extending her life, the Monarch Queen was able to inspire her followers for the duration of the migration. The butterflies shared the harmony and goodwill that fairies and pixies brought to Eludia.

Though butterflies were comfortable with fairies and pixies, not all creatures were. Even after living with the fairies and pixies for eons, the Eludian animals were naturally cautious around the mystical beings. Eludians called fairies and pixies, "Wonderfolke," with the original name being "wander folke." The name came from Eludians who felt the fairies and pixies had "wandered" into Eludia uninvited.

That is why the butterflies' message of harmony was so important–it opened the door for peace when paths did cross between fairies and pixies and Eludian creatures.

During the Emergence, the Monarch Queen's position of leadership, and thus her message, was strengthened when she was taught to fly with *majesty*. Every butterfly knew how to fly once they transitioned from the chrysalis, but few had the natural gift of leadership. Majesty provided the Monarch Queen leadership skills so she could guide her followers.

Po's grasp brought Marri Golde back to the moment. His conch-shell-colored fingers pressed gently into her light-green arm. It was not painful; his touch was warm, yet urgent.

Marri Golde's knees had buckled from the prospect of leaving their home tree and pursuing the very thing they always wanted–a child of their own. Someone who would be the summation of their love, who could understand their love. The hope was all-encompassing.

The fairy melted into her husband's chest. The shimmering translucence of their wings enveloped the pixie and fairy. Po carefully placed one arm between his wife's wings and slipped the other under her knees. The pixie carried his love to their mattress stuffed with hummingbird down, laying her on her side, so her wings did not tangle. Once she was comfortable, Po used a finger to brush a single strand of hair out of his love's blue eyes.

"We must bring forth a child, Mare," the pixie said quietly. "This is the only way."

♦

Marri Golde knew she would not be able to lead the ritual of the Emergence forever. She needed a child of her own to whom she could pass on her family's gift. Every night before bed, the fairy whispered those very desires to the Weeping Tree.

Marri Golde had prayed for a child her entire adult life, but now was the time to elevate the Weeping Tree's will into action. She and Po had to make the trek to Tree Hill to see the Weeping Tree. The Luna family needed an heiress to perform the ritual.

Many troupes in Homestead had children of their own, including a mix in numbers and genders. The Luna troupe was always blessed with a child, though there was no mystery to how many offspring they might have or if their children would be male, female, or non-assigned. The Luna family was always blessed with exactly one little girl. As the young fairy matured into adulthood and formed a familial troupe of her own, the Luna name was always maintained to show respect to the importance of the Emergence.

Marri Golde's most cherished memory from the Emergence was the moment her mother, Hildeburre, first handed control of the ritual to her as a young fairy. Marri Golde did not know she was ready until she was actually in the presence of the Monarch Queen. That moment bonded mother and newly adult child more deeply than ever before.

This memory was always present in Marri Golde's mind. And when Marri Golde and Po left Homestead and moved to Milkweed Fields, it was because of her name that the couple was able to exist outside Homestead until they found the right home tree. The Elder Tree of the woods where the fairy and pixie resided had recognized the Luna name and given her and Po temporary protection while the two were in the woods of the Elder Tree. The fairy and pixie were able to deliberate safely in their search for a home tree.

To become a home tree, a tree had to be strong, consistent, and loyal to the familial troupe. It was not a responsibility to be taken lightly. It was an honor bestowed upon only the most reputable Eludian trees.

The trees themselves could not tell the difference between fairies and pixies, for it did not matter if a fairy troupe or a pixie troupe bestowed the honor of becoming a home tree. All Eludians, including trees, viewed fairies and pixies the same way: as Wonderfolke. To be chosen to serve the Wonderfolke had become a privilege.

At the beginning, the feeling was that the fairies and pixies were intruding on Eludia, but as the name transformed from "wander folke" to "Wonderfolke," so too did the feelings Eludians had towards fairies and pixies. Because of the butterflies' message of good will, Eludians were open to Wonderfolke, even if they could not distinguish between the two types of beings.

Fairies and pixies certainly knew the difference between themselves. Pixies were tall and connected to the physical world. Their strongest sense was touch. By comparison, fairies were smaller, quicker, and more agile. Their shades of greens stood in stark contrast to the pinks and paisleys of pixies. Where pixies were clever with their hands, a fairy's strongest sense was empathy.

Eludian creatures could not tell the difference between fairies and pixies because all Wonderfolke have the same language. Each Eludian creature knew two languages: "Eludian" and their native tongue. Fairies and pixies spoke the same native tongue.

Eludian was the common tongue. It was developed in the days of old to accommodate the various speaking styles of Eludia's creatures. It was simple, but everyone in Eludia understood it and could communicate with it.

By comparison, native tongues were based on the particular speaking style of each Eludian creature. Each dialect took into account tongues, lips, beaks, teeth, or the lack thereof. Because of this, native tongues were only understood by creatures of the same type. Native tongues were still in use because they allowed creatures of a similar type to communicate privately.

For example, if a butterfly wanted to talk to a squirrel, the two could through Eludian. But if a butterfly was talking to another butterfly and did not want other creatures to listen in on their private conversation, the two butterflies could speak Butterfloid to one another. Butterfloid was the natural language of butterflies. Though all types of butterflies spoke Butterfloid, no other creature could understand it.

There were, however, three exceptions: pixies could communicate with mammals, birds, and fish. Fairies could talk to the ancient animals, such as reptiles, amphibians, and insects. And trees could communicate with all creatures (but often choose not to). Trees communicated through thought. Since thoughts do not have the barriers of beaks, teeth, or gums, trees understood all languages.

But this knowledge was old knowledge. These three exceptions had been long forgotten five hundred years ago–until just after Marri Golde had turned one hundred. When the change was made, the Grand Troupe Council encouraged all Wonderfolke to only speak in Eludian to non-Wonderfolke, except during ceremony. The Grand Troupe Council said they wanted fairies and pixies to be a greater part of the community. The native tongues were still taught to young fairies and pixies; Wonderfolke just were not encouraged to use them outside of Homestead.

As generations of creatures and trees transitioned, so did the memory of Wonderfolke understanding native tongues. It had been so long, only the Home Trees and the Wonderfolke recalled those days. And the Home Trees spoke to no one about the Wonderfolke.

As a young oak tree, Nahke could not feel the difference between fairies and pixies. It was Nahke, however, who rediscovered the Wonderfolke's forgotten secret of understanding other Eludian languages. And by keeping that secret, it was why he became the Home Tree of Marri Golde and Po.

♦

Before they became the Home Tree of Po and Marri Golde about four hundred years ago, Nahke was a young oak tree living near the milkweed fields southeast of Homestead. They knew Wonderfolke were nearby, but Nahke had not seen these specific creatures yet.

Nahke also knew most Wonderfolke traveled to the fields on the day of the Emergence, but the Wonderfolke's ceremony had occurred three moon cycles earlier. To have Wonderfolke visit Milkweed Fields now was very unusual. Because of this, Nahke began to listen a little more intently to the animals who gossiped in the oak tree's shade, hoping to gain some insight. They wanted to gain as much understanding of anyone who came to Milkweed Fields. If danger presented itself in the data Nahke collected, the young oak could send messages through the animals and insects who visited to ensure the safety of the Milkweed Fields community.

It was odd for two Wonderfolke to be in the area. More so, these two had been around for a while and Nahke heard from the squirrels that the Wonderfolke had decided to stay. The two had asked the eldest tree of the forest near Milkweed Fields if the couple could settle into the hollow of a fallen tree for an "extended period of time." The Elder Tree had given a blessing.

But then, Nahke overheard something they had not heard before. The oak heard a horned lark share the secret of an insect with another horned lark. Nahke's branches immediately rustled. Larks ate insects; they did not talk to them, and certainly not in their native tongue–the language of secrets. Nahke filed the information away.

The two Wonderfolke stayed in Milkweed Fields–in that hollow on the outskirts of the forest–for over twenty years. They primarily kept to themselves, but something unusual happened when the Emergence arrived; the two Wonderfolke departed. Once the Emergence was over, however, the two re-emerged in the hollow. It was unusual because typically the opposite happened–all the Wonderfolke in Eludia traveled to Milkweed Fields for the ceremony. It was stranger still that their absence went on for years.

Perhaps the two were searching for a Home Tree after all, mused Nahke.

Then, a few years after the first odd event of the lark knowing the secret of an insect, it happened again. This time, Nahke witnessed a badger sharing the secret of a toad, and again, badgers do not speak toad. They eat them. Despite the time that had elapsed, the events were so odd that Nahke connected them immediately.

A lark and insect; a badger and toad? It had to be someone who understood multiple native tongues, thought Nahke. *Only someone who understood multiple Eludian languages would be able to talk to a lark and an insect and a badger and a toad. The secrets of animals were only shared in their native language. That meant it was either a talkative tree (which was blasphemy), or it had something to do with the Wonderfolke who were a-wing in the milkweed fields. The Wonderfolke were the only change in an otherwise normal season.*

A year later, Nahke confirmed their suspicions when they observed the Wonderfolke start a conversation with a flock of sparrow. The sparrows filled the branches of a nearby maple tree. To prompt the conversation, the Wonderfolke began with questions about local trees. Unsurprisingly, no meaningful responses resulted from the flock. One of the Wonderfolke offered a bit of gossip about crickets. The sparrows perked up, but they ultimately remained silent on trees.

The Wonderfolke thanked the sparrows, and they slowly flitted away.

As soon as the Wonderfolke turned their wings, the chatter of the birds leapt to life and the flock pecked at the cricket gossip before moving on to the juicier interest of local trees. Because they spoke in their native tongue, each sparrow shared their honest thoughts.

Nahke noted that the Wonderfolke had flitted away at first, but they had not landed too far from the flock. Nahke observed the taller Wonderfolke cock his head intently as the sparrows chattered, and then every so often, the taller Wonderfolke would whisper something to the smaller one.

If one had not been paying attention, most would have thought the two Wonderfolke were just having a chat. Nahke, however, filtered the conversation through everything they had heard. Suddenly, Nahke became convinced the bigger Wonderfolke was translating Birdling to the slender one.

Nahke was elated—*they had figured out that the Wonderfolke understood multiple Eludian languages!*—but the oak tree immediately purged themselves of the thought. Even if the oak tree was right and the Wonderfolke were able to listen in on conversations, Nahke did not feel it was their place to share their hunch with anyone. It simply was not their news to share. Trees were meant to listen.

This characteristic was what set Nahke apart from the other trees. Most young trees were focused on reaching the sky, but Nahke was committed to extending their roots. They dug into the hilltop, gave birds safe harbor, and fed the Eludian creatures acorns. Nahke was no longer a sapling, but their ability to listen and not share what they heard, was what was so special about the young oak.

Years later, Nahke discovered Marri Golde and Po had purposely had the conversation with the sparrows within sight of the young oak tree. The Wonderfolke knew a smart tree would discover their secret, but a reputable tree would not share it.

"Nahke," smiled Marri Golde years after they had first met. "We listened in on the Eludian conversations in their native tongues. Never once was there even a hint that you were not an honest and good tree. You are strong and silent, Nahke. That's why we picked you as our Home Tree."

On Marri Golde's two hundred and twenty-fifth birthday, the fairy and her husband inducted Nahke into their familial troupe. The ceremony was just the three of them, but it officially bonded the oak tree to the troupe of the Wonderfolke. Nahke was sworn to protect their familial troupe against all enemies.

In exchange for Nahke's service, Marri Golde and Po each removed a piece of their wing and gifted it to the young oak tree. The possession of Wonderfolke wings extended the life of the oak tree tenfold. Now, Nahke would live to be 1,004 years old.

Nahke never wavered once. They had seen their fair share of marauders—crow, Hoo bird, and ferocious bear—and Nahke had succeeded in hiding the Wonderfolke from these creatures.

These creatures sought to possess Wonderfolke wings above all things.

Crows wanted the wings for their life-lengthening abilities. Hoo birds sought them for their stored wisdom. Bears found them to be delicious.

Because of this, Nahke not only learned how to hide the presence of Wonderfolke, but they also proved useful when searching for information. Nahke almost always was one of the first to hear news, any news. They heard rumors in the throats of birds, the wings of insects, and on the tongues of mammals.

When the Grand Troupe summoned Wonderfolke for the Emergence, the banished were excluded unless they were called by name. When called by name, each fairy or pixie had to respond to the summons or surrender their wings. Nahke always heard the names; Marri Golde was called every year. By agreement, so was Po.

It had not always been that way. The couple went without seeing any Wonderfolke for years, and even then, they only saw an occasional Wonderfolke who wandered through Milkweed Fields unexpectedly.

The Emergence, however, had become the answer to Marri Golde's whispers. She valued the time with other Wonderfolke, but the fairy felt Po needed the connection with other fairies and pixies more than ever before. Their once-a-year summons was a gift from the Weeping Tree.

Po brushed the hair behind his wife's ear, bringing Marri Golde back to the present. They were in the comfort of Nahke, their home tree.

"Nahke can help us find our way. They can tap into the old knowledge and teach us how to ask the Weeping Tree for a gift. We must go, Mare."

◆

After Nahke became their home tree, Marri Golde, Po, and the oak tree lived together near the Milkweed Fields, undisturbed, for over one hundred years. This was a period of isolation for the fairy and pixie. Each spring when the Emergence occurred, Nahke would hide the Wonderfolke until the Grand Troupe had come and gone from Milkweed Fields.

The names of Marri Golde and Po were never called during this period, but the fairy knew her mother was nearby, leading the ceremony.

Despite her mother being one of the oldest fairies in Homestead, Hildeburre was now the Luna troupe's youngest adult female who was in good standing with the Grand Troupe Council. With Marri Golde's banishment, Hildeburre was now, once again, asked to lead the Emergence.

That all changed on Marri Golde's three hundred and twenty-ninth birthday when Nahke received word of Hildeburre's passing. With her transition from this world to the next and Marri Golde's banishment, there was no one left in Homestead to perform the Emergence.

Hildebrund–Hildeburre's husband–knew his daughter was Homestead's only hope; Marri Golde was the last female from the Luna troupe. However, Hildebrund was doubtful the Grand Troupe Council would ever consider asking his daughter to return. Her sin was too egregious.

In fact, Hildebrund was right. The Grand Troupe Council was indignant at the thought of welcoming Marri Golde back to conduct the ceremony. The fairy had been banished for the most heinous of crimes: intermarriage. If they invited her back, her example could lead to chaos amongst fairies and pixies. What if other fairies and pixies were to wed? The thought was too terrible to bear.

Instead, the Council defiantly performed the ceremony themselves. They had been preparing for this moment. Their first Emergence was hailed a success by the Council.

However, that following spring, barely half of the Monarch Queen's followers returned to the Milkweed Fields. The Council worked furiously to refine their ritual, but it took until the following spring to interpret the results.

Again, disaster.

Each year, the followers diminished, and each year the message of the Wonderfolke's goodwill reached fewer and fewer Eludians. By the time the fourth migration had occurred, it was the smallest on record in nearly two millennia. Eludia was destabilizing.

The Crow King of the time, Gigantor III, saw an opportunity to expand the crow's territory and cawed his legion of black birds out of Dark Forest and into a battle with the fairies and pixies.

The war lasted five years, only ending when the Wonderfolke joined forces with the willder bees. The bees had also been tormented by the Crow King's expansion. Together, Wonderfolke and willder bee pushed Gigantor III and his murder of crows back into Dark Forest.

Many on both sides lost their wings, including Marri Golde's father Hildebrund and both of Po's parents. However, because of their banishment, the names of Marri Golde and Po were not called by the Grand Troupe Council for their parents' transition ceremonies.

When the crows were forced back to Dark Forest, the Council turned their focus to rebuilding harmony. There was tremendous pressure from the familial troupes to lift Marri Golde's banishment, and for the fairy to lead the Emergence once again.

Decades marched by, but the Council finally relented to the pressure and considered the option of calling Marri Golde's name. A party of six—three pixie, three fairy—traveled to Milkweed Fields to recruit the last remaining member of the Luna troupe.

"Ms. Marri Golde of the great Luna's," began the Lead Deacon upon their arrival. He was a heavyset pixie with sunset-pink coloring. "The Council does not know how long peace can be maintained with the crows. As the last remaining Luna troupe member, we ask of you . . ."

Po coughed.

"We plead with you," continued the Senior Warden, gracefully fluttering to the front. The Senior Warden was tall for a fairy and possessed a deep toad-green hue. He was the leader of the contingent visiting from Homestead. "We request you lead the Emergence each spring. Without the Monarch Queen's goodwill, we do not know how long peace can be maintained."

"Each spring?" Po blurted in. "Lead the Emergence? Are we even welcome in Homestead again?"

"The Wonderfolke, Po," the Lead Deacon stammered. "Think of the Wonderfolke."

"What about us?" Po fluttered his wings, hovering with an angry buzz. He and his wife had been banished for hundreds of years. And now that Homestead needed Marri Golde, they had come back to their troupe, asking for help. Po couldn't believe it. The Senior Warden shot a glare at the Lead Deacon, just as Marri Golde flew up to her husband, calming Po.

Once all had settled, Marri Golde turned to the Council and addressed the Senior Warden.

"I hear your request. I need time to talk this over with my troupe." The Lead Deacon tripped his wings angrily at the thought of a fairy and pixie being in the same troupe. Po chitted his wings in return. The Senior Warden quieted both with a quick staccato blast, and Marri Golde continued, "Return in one moon cycle and I will give you my decision."

Once the Council left, Po exploded.

"Only now they want us back? Only now? Over one hundred years of isolation. Not seeing the passing of all four of our parents. It's cost us too much, Mare. It's cost us too much."

But Marri Golde knew this was their opportunity to be a part of Homestead again. With Po's parents now gone and no children of their own, Marri Golde did not want her husband isolated if she were to transition first. The isolation during the crow wars was hard enough on their troupe. The fairy pleaded with her husband.

"We must, Po. If we don't help, all Eludia could enter a period of disharmony that could endanger every Eludian creature, especially the Wonderfolke. If I perform the Emergence, the Monarch Queen's followers will spread goodwill about fairies and pixies across all of Eludia. This will ensure war is not seen for the life of a Home Tree."

"They treat us like snails, Mare," the pixie fumed. "Common garden snails. Why do we bother?"

"It is a start, Po," urged the fairy. "All we need is a way to show our love is true love, and then we'll both be embraced." Marri Golde believed it was a beginning. If she helped the Grand Troupe Council, it could be a way back into the community.

Po saw the determination in his wife's eyes and knew she was right. Po nodded his head slowly at first, then picked up speed. Marri Golde rushed to her husband's side, and they enveloped one another in their wings.

Being welcomed back for the Emergence was only a start. Marri Golde knew the road to reconnection with the Homestead was for her and Po to have a child. A newborn would give the Homestead hope the Emergence would be secure for a millennia and tie Po more closely to the greater troupe.

When the Grand Troupe Council returned, Marri Golde agreed to lead the Emergence, and Po stood by his wife. Marri Golde led the Emergence each spring and Po's name was called alongside hers. It had been over 228 years since Marri Golde had first led the Emergence, but now, the Homestead's most sacred ritual was once again led by the Luna troupe.

◆

Over a quarter of a millennium after being asked to lead the Emergence once again, Marri Golde realized she was closer to her own transition from this world than she was to the first time she'd performed the Emergence. She and Po were both over six hundred years old, and yet they still had no child of their own.

Concerned the unstable peace with the Crow King would erupt into war if an heiress was not found, Marri Golde had partnered with the Council to teach the strongest and smartest young fairies the ritual of the Emergence. Marri Golde focused on the fairies because they spoke Butterfloid, where the pixies could not. Being able to speak in the butterflies' native tongue was critical: the intimacy of their own dialect meant the Monarch Queen would be more apt to trust the voice she was hearing.

For two and a half centuries, Marri Golde had worked alongside every fairy the Grand Troupe Council sent to her. Marri Golde sensed Po enjoyed seeing the new faces, but the fairy was frustrated that she had not yet found an heiress. Some of her pupils were strong and others were smart, but none had the combination of courage, empathy, and teamwork needed to teach majesty properly. The fairy knew she had to find an heiress elsewhere. She just did not know how.

"Nahke," the fairy lamented to the home tree one summer evening. Marri Golde sprawled in the uppermost limbs of the tree. "I've taught every young fairy the rites of the Emergence, and yet, no one has what's needed to teach majesty consistently. Whenever I hand the ceremony over to a student, she stumbles on the ritual, collapses under the physical strain, or she can't adapt to something unexpected. I need to find an heiress, Nahke. I need an heiress to learn the gift of my family–to teach the Monarch Queen majesty."

Nahke listened, as home trees usually do. The oak was always listening, especially when the Wonderfolke spoke. After some contemplation, Nahke finally exchanged their thoughts with the Marri Golde.

Ms. Marri Golde, offered the home tree, *generations ago, the ancient animals spoke of the Weeping Tree and her ability to answer whispers.*

"Yes," the fairy replied, playing mindlessly with a leaf, barely holding on to Nahke's most out-stretched limb. "I send my whispers to the Weeping Tree each night. But nothing, Nahke. It's still just the three of us. You, me, and Po."

It's not enough to want something, Mare, the oak replied thoughtfully. *One must put in the work to earn it.*

The fairy stopped playing with the leaf, cocked her head, and asked, "What do you mean, you old log? I'm happy to work hard for it. I've been teaching the Homesteaders my secret since the crow wars."

It's not enough. You must go.

"Go." Marri Golde wanted to be mad, but she knew that was the only way. She knew if she were to transition to the next world without an heiress, the current Crow King might rally his murder of crows and attack again.

Moreso, Marri Golde knew if she were to pass without a child, her husband's connection to Homestead would be severed and his name would never be called again. The Grand Troupe Council only tolerated Po because of his relationship with Marri Golde and her troupe's relationship with the Emergence. Without the link through ritual, Po was sure to be lost on his own.

Was Nahke right? Would the Weeping Tree answer her whispers if she were to present them herself?

"Nahke. Are the stories about the Weeping Tree true?"

There are many stories about the Weeping Tree, thought Nahke to Marri Golde, *but there are only a few consistencies from the old stories to now. Assuming those consistencies are truth, then this is what I have gathered to be true about the Weeping Tree.*

The fairy leaned forward.

First, the Weeping Tree sits atop Tree Hill.

Second, when Moon is not in the sky, she sleeps in the hollow of the Weeping Tree. Sun does the same when he is not racing across the blue.

Third, the Weeping Tree will hear your wish, but only when she is alone.

Nahke paused.

"That's it?" the fairy eventually asked.

Nahke did not respond.

"How can I see the Weeping Tree alone if the Moon or Sun are always in her hollow?" Marri Golde furrowed her brow. Her jaw clenched and her teeth seesawed, grinding away doubt.

Suddenly, her mouth fell agape, and a wide grin spread across her face.

"That's it, Nahke. I know when to visit the Weeping Tree."

The oak did not respond.

"Nahke, can you tell me when the next eclipse is?"

Ah yes, murmured Nahke, impressed with the fairy. *The next solar eclipse is in four days.*

Marri Golde sat up straight. Then the fairy bent and kissed the limb she sat on. She rushed inside the hollow of the home tree to find Po.

Once inside, Marri Golde found Po quickly and told him what Nahke had shared with her. Their whispers could be answered. They could still have a child of their own.

"We must go," Po responded when she was done recanting the story. He held her arm gently, but firmly. Overcome by emotion, Marri Golde collapsed. Po lifted her and laid her on the bed stuffed in hummingbird down.

Marri Golde eventually lifted herself from the mattress and said, "Yes, my love. Let's go."

♦

Po knew he and Marri Golde had to reach the top of Tree Hill by the time the solar eclipse was at its height. There was no choice.

Nahke had relayed stories of expeditions to Tree Hill, but the stories did nothing to shed light on the dangers. Po was betting not just the life of his wife, but the entire future of Wonderfolke. The pixie could feel not just his troupe, but the entire Grand Troupe, pushing him and Marri Golde up Tree Hill.

Homestead needed an heiress for The Emergence, and by Moon and Sun above, Po was going to do his part.

It took three days for Marri Golde and Po to be within striking distance of Tree Hill's summit. They traveled across Eludia and had passed over shale, cracks, and chasms, pushing through howling winds that forced them to walk and briar patches that tore at their clothes and skin.

Today, the skies were a cold, steel blue. The Weeping Tree perched far out ahead of them.

We must go now, Po told himself. *We must reach Tree Hill by the time Moon leaves to join the Sun during the eclipse.*

Po kissed his wife awake. She was exhausted from the trip so he had let her sleep a little longer this last morning. He needed her rested, but they needed to cross this last part of the journey in unity with the heavens.

Eludia's temperatures rarely fluctuated, but as they got closer to the summit, Po and Marri Golde began to shiver. The two pulled taut every strand of chrysalis they had on them. Po tightened his green and black kilt, and Marri Golde pulled a little tighter her lavender open-back dress.

"Mare, we have to keep moving," Po turned his face out of the wind and squinted back at Marri Golde. "We have to reach the top by the time of the eclipse. It's our only way the Weeping Tree will hear our pleas without the influence of Moon and Sun."

Marri Golde nodded. She wrapped her purple scarf and wings around her. The winds were too strong to fly, but at least her wings and scarf protected the fairy from the elements. They pushed on.

A short while later, Po could see the peak of the tree at the crest of the mountain. He did not want to approach too early, so he kept himself and Marri Golde out of sight by hiding in a bush that had been battered by the elements.

A short while later, it happened. Even with Sun sitting at his highest point, the sky began to darken. Birds sang their goodnights and crickets joined in chorus. The winds quieted. An eerie peace and odd glow slowly overtook Eludia. The pixie and fairy had never seen anything so beautiful.

"Now, Mare. *Now*," Po urged quietly yet firmly. "Don't let their union blind you. We have to make it to the willow while Moon and Sun are gone."

Po straightened his kilt and grasped his wife's hand. He chirped his wings in assurance and Marri Golde clipped back. Together, they took advantage of the quieted winds and flew over the crest to face what came next.

The Weeping Tree's very presence was simultaneously welcoming and humbling, her graceful crown of branches swept to the ground in a seemingly deferential bow to all who came to see her. Her green-yellow hue soothed the soul. Despite being alone, surrounded only by danger, the ancient willow was a glorious welcome for all those who witnessed her firsthand. She smelled of hope.

The couple was overcome. The fairy and pixie could fly no more. Instead, they fell to the earth and began to weep. It had taken them days to reach her, and yet, their most star-struck vision of the Weeping Tree was obliterated by her authentic beauty. Marri Golde and Po fell to their knees, clasping onto one another.

Out of nowhere, a wind stirred and blew in from the east. The Weeping Tree's branches opened and the couple saw warmth within. The lovestruck couple rose to their feet and stumbled out of the temporary night and through the parted branches. Their nerves were muted by the cool winds and the energy that was drawing them into the Weeping Tree.

Once inside, the wind stopped and the tree closed around them. The warmth of her protection encouraged them to share their deepest wants.

Marri Golde and Po threw themselves at the willow's roots and pleaded desperately for a child. They each tore off a small piece of their wing and buried it in the earth at the base of the tree as an offering. They lay in front of the willow, whispering their unified desire.

As they lay on their stomachs in front of the Weeping Tree, a silver baby's hand pushed through the dirt at the base of the tree. Marri Golde could not believe her eyes. Could it be? Could their whispers be heard so quickly?

Po knew immediately what was happening: if the Weeping Tree was going to help, she had to move before Moon returned.

Po and Marri Golde carefully, but quickly, dug around the baby's hand, revealing an arm, then a body and a head, then tiny legs the width of a cricket's whiskers. But when the baby's tiny silver wings were free from the earth, Po and Marri Golde burst into tears–wings are the tell-tale sign of Wonderfolke. The baby was not pink like a pixie or green like a fairy. She was silver like the lining of a cloud and her eyes were a rich earthen-brown. Her wings were a subtle silver, but when they chirped, they carried a shimmering array of color. Marri Golde had never seen wings so beautiful.

"Elphie," Marri Golde cooed. "Her name is Elphie Askul."

Po gazed upon the child and knew that was her name.

"Po, our whispers have been answered. Look, she's Wonderfolke. She must be half-fairy, half-pixie, one hundred percent Wonderfolke. She's a 'fixie,' Po. She's made of us."

Po did not know what to say, but if the Weeping Tree was offering them a child, who was he to deny the gift. Po's thinking was more for the safety of his wife and their newly found child. Moon would be returning to the willow shortly, and if Po knew anything, he knew it was best they not be there when she arrived. Po swept up the baby and handed her to Marri Golde. The fairy wrapped her purple scarf around the silver child.

Just then, the willow's branches opened and Po could see the midnight skies lightening. Po turned to his wife, "We must go."

Marri Golde kissed Elphie's forehead, then nodded to Po. Without looking back, the two chittered their wings and flew as hard and as far as they could. Around them, a false dawn broke; birds sung their hello's. Marri Golde and Po both knew Moon was returning home.

As the brief night became day again, the winds resumed, and Marri Golde and Po were forced to land and take to foot. Po took Elphie and the new family pushed onward.

It took five days to return to Nahke, but they did so with their child. Now they had another living creature to tend to, a child of their own. The Emergence was saved. Elphie Askul had arrived.

The Crow Kueen

Elphie Askul hated being different. She was not quite as tall as the graceful pixies and was slower than the quicker fairies. Her skin and wings did not have the translucent tones of others in her family. Instead, Elphie's coloring was a shimmering silver. Even her eyes were different. Instead of the pixies' green or the fairies' blue, Elphie's eyes were an earth-rich brown that did not seem anything like any of the Wonderfolke she knew.

Elphie's parents loved her nonetheless. Her father Po, a pixie with deep conch shell coloring and moss-green eyes, was 711 years old. He stood a towering six inchworms, had thimble-broad shoulders, and a voice as deep as a field mouse. His wife Marri Golde, already shorter than the blossoming Elphie, was the color of lily pads and as thin as a blade of grass. She had aqua-blue eyes the shape of a morning dew drop. Marri Golde was a vibrant 705 years old.

Nahke was a little younger. The 555-year-old oak tree rounded out Elphie's familial troupe. They were strong and silent, but they were also Elphie's greatest teacher. The old oak tree had shared with Elphie the old knowledge, as well as what was important to the animals and trees of today. Elphie was impatient when learning, in part because she wanted to explore, and in part because she was Nahke's only pupil so all the attention was always on her. Regardless, everything was being done to ensure Elphie was ready for the Emergence as soon as she turned one hundred.

In Eludia, it was forbidden for fairies and pixies to have children together, yet nearly one hundred years ago Marri Golde and Po had made the journey to the Weeping Tree. Nahke had told her that in the very center of Eludia the ancient willow tree stood atop Tree Hill. Surrounded by chasms and ravines, the tree was isolated from all those not strong enough to make the journey. When Moon and Sun were not in the sky, the hollow of this wise old tree was where the two each spent their time. From the tree, Moon and Sun could see all of Eludia. Elphie was brought home from the weeping tree nearly one hundred years before.

A fairy or pixie's one hundredth birthday was significant for Wonderfolke, as that was when they were given permission to use their wings. It's not that fairies and pixies can't fly before they are one hundred; it's that they are not allowed to, as flying can be treacherous.

Elphie was ninety-nine–*and a quarter*–and desperately wanted to earn her wings. Even though it was forbidden, the impatient Elphie had been traveling to Far Meadow to secretly practice. Elphie jumped off any rock she could find in the broad, flat grasslands, launching into the air to chase mosquitoes and bumble bees. She had not flown very high and was not very fast, but she had become pretty agile, catching her first dragonfly just recently. The young fixie found flight to be exhilarating.

It was a long walk to the meadow, but Elphie had befriended a hedgehog by the name of Ryart. Ryart was smaller than the other hedgehogs in his den, but he was lightning quick. Moreover, Ryart often played in the woods by himself, so he knew the shortcuts through Eludia better than anyone. If you needed to get somewhere fast, Ryart was your hedgehog. Despite knowing the Luna family only had one child each generation, Elphie had always wanted a kid brother or sister, and Ryart was the next best thing–her best friend.

He and Elphie had met under odd circumstances but had hit it off right away. Ryart had been eying Elphie's father's grub garden–the most delicious in Eludia. Instead of telling Papa, Elphie had struck up a conversation with the young hedgehog. The animals in Eludia knew their own language but could only speak the common Eludian language to each other. Fairies and pixies, on the other wing, could understand creatures in their native tongue. Only the crows were resistant to the message of good will and Elphie had been told to stay well clear of those types of birds. Even with being able to speak to many creatures, Elphie knew fairies and pixies often chose to not speak to the animals. The Wonderfolke she had met at the Emergence, though, liked to listen in on the secrets of Eludian creatures.

Elphie, however, had sauntered right up to Ryart and said, "Hello, Mister Hedgehog, what's your name?" Ryart had been caught completely off guard, both because he had picked out a yummy-looking grub, and because Elphie's Hedgehonian was pretty good.

The two struck up a fast friendship that had lasted through two winters. When Elphie shared she wanted to fly by her upcoming spring birthday, Ryart thought of the perfect private location: Far Meadow.

"No one, and I mean no one, ever goes out there because you have to go through Dark Forest to get there," Ryart warned. "But I can get us there safely because I can zoom. Jump on my back and hold on tight, Elphie!"

Elphie may have been small for a pixie, but she was the right size for a hedgehog. She climbed onto her friend, and they zoomed through the woods.

Ryart always took the quickest route. To determine where north was, when he woke up each morning, he would stand tall, with his right shoulder toward the rising sun. He knew he was facing north when his shadow fell directly to his left.

Later in the day, Ryart verified north by checking the moss at the base of trees. Moss often grew on the side of the tree with the least amount of sun, and in most cases, that was north. Using the moss, the lightning-fast hedgehog navigated Eludia during the day.

At night, Ryart used the North Star to find his way. First, he would scan the sky for the Big Dipper. He knew what a dipper was because he had seen Elphie use one to "dip" nectar out of flowers. Once he found it, he found the two stars that the nectar would have run off if the dipper was tipped; he knew the North Star was always five times the distance away from the tip of the dipper. He just had to draw from the bottom pointer to the top pointer and go in that direction. True north was almost directly under this star.

Elphie and Ryart had been traveling to Far Meadow for a long time, and today was no different. Once Elphie finished feeding her family's beetle, she checked in with her mother to see if she was free to explore Eludia. Her mother was in Nahke's main hollow, weaving dandelions and chrysalis into a rug.

"Now, be careful Elphie," her mother urged.

The fixie shifted from foot to foot. Marri Golde gazed sternly at Elphie until she became still. Once her daughter had quieted, the fairy continued.

"Before you go, please water the baby rosemary and check the thyme in the gardens east of Nahke. Once you've finished, you are free to adventure with Ryart."

"Thank you, Mama!" The fixie quickly kissed her mother and turned to go.

"Just be home by dark, Love," Marri Golde warned.

"Of course, Mama!" Elphie said over her shoulder as she climbed out of Nahke. She fluttered her wings, pretending to fly, as she climbed down Nahke's trunk. Once she was on the ground, she brushed off her blue dress made of chrysalis, straightened her satchel, and skipped off to the garden.

Once her chores were done, Elphie selected a mushroom stem for herself from the nearby cluster, then swung by the grub garden, picked out two plump ones, and dropped them into her bag. Elphie ran to the outskirts of milkweed fields to meet Ryart.

"I've got something for you, Ry! Two big fat ones!"

"Good!" shouted the hedgehog. "Get on. I'll have you to Far Meadow in no time."

Ryart crossed over Deep Creek where it was narrowest, skirted through the edges of Dark Forest, and arrived in Far Meadow. The scent of lavender was subtle.

Far Meadow is in the east of Eludia. The never-ending grassland is sprinkled with stones of varying sizes. It sits just over Deep Creek, on the other side of Dark Forest. Po warned Elphie repeatedly about the crows who resided in the dank woods. The birds were the enemy of fairies and pixies.

Ryart pulled up next to a giant rock they had found just yesterday. It loomed over the tips of the long, thin grass and was almost as high as the nearby heavy heads of sunflowers. Elphie opened her satchel and selected the larger grub to hand to her friend.

Looks delicious, he thought. *Elphie always finds the fattest.*

Fearlessly, Elphie climbed to the top of the rock while Ryart turned his grub over and over in his paws.

"Ryart, look at me! Look how high I am. I'm going to *fly!*"

Ryart barely peered up from his snack. "Good luck, Elphie!"

Elphie put out her arms, closed her eyes, fluttered her wings, and jumped.

But just as she was dropping, she was snatched out of the air by a giant crow. Ryart peeked up in time to see the big black bird grab Elphie mid-flight. Ryart dropped his grub and jumped to his feet.

"Elphie! *Elphie!*"

Ryart saw Elphie pass out in the clutches of the bird. He watched the crow take her into the Dark Forest. Ryart zoomed after his friend.

◆

Ryart was fast enough to catch the crow, but he stayed hidden. He wanted to find out exactly where the bird was taking Elphie. When they reached the edge of the wood, the black bird flew to a large, scraggly nest in a tall, dead pine tree. Ryart ducked behind nearby bushes to examine the scene.

The bird's home was most of the way up the tree. The pine loomed above everything except for a nearby redwood. The crow's nest was a haphazard jumble of decorations glittering with shiny bits of gold and silver-colored items, more than Ryart had ever seen in one place. He could not pick out which piece of silver was Elphie, but he was positive he had followed the crow to the right place.

His best friend was up there; he had to figure out a way to get her down before dark. If he did not, Marri Golde and Po would ground Elphie for another one hundred years.

"How am I going to save her?" he wondered aloud.

The crow hopped to the branch above the nest, then disappeared out of sight. Ryart could not fly or climb trees, so he did not know what to do.

Just then an unidentified flying object swooped above his head. Ryart ducked before gathering himself. Was it a crow? Or the dreaded Hoo bird? Ryart may be a small hedgehog, but he was fierce. He scanned the sky, readying to protect himself.

"Bonjour, Friend," said a creature in perfect Eludian dialect. Ryart turned and came face-to-face with a squirrel. Or he thought she was a squirrel. She seemed . . . different.

Ryart squinted. She wore a gold necklace and rings on her fingers. He sniffed. She smelled like a squirrel, but she also smelled like green apples and cinnamon. Ryart licked the air with his tongue. She even tasted like a squirrel. But she had flown over his head.

"Who are you?" asked Ryart.

"Moi? Why, I'm the Magnificent Flying Frances. But you can call me Jewels," she said with a wink. "Who are you?"

"I'm Ryart, the hedgehog. What are you?"

"Why, I'm the Greatest Show on Earth," laughed Jewels.

Ryart cocked his head, perplexed. "Aren't you a squirrel?"

"Au contraire, my little friend. I am not just a squirrel. I am a *flying* squirrel." Jewels beamed broadly.

"So, you're a squirrel," responded Ryart.

"No, no, no. Not a common grey squirrel or even the rare black squirrel. I am a . . ." Jewels paused for effect, then leaned in. "A *flying* squirrel."

"Squirrels can't fly. I've seen 1,029 of them. They jump," Ryart stated flatly.

Undeterred, Jewels extended her arms, lifting them over her head. She revealed what looked like flaps of skin attached between her arms and her sides. "Voilà!" Jewels exclaimed.

Those could be wings, Ryart mused, *but they don't seem like any I've seen before.*

"Well, if you can fly, can you help me get my friend down? She's up in the crow's nest."

Jewels craned her neck up at the bird's home glittering in the early afternoon sun.

"My friend Elphie is up there," continued the hedgehog. "I need to get her down before it gets too late. We live on the other side of Eludia, and her mother wants her home before dark."

"Oh, I see," said the flying squirrel. "Well, typically, I just come to this part of Eludia to shop for jewelry. The crows, well, they have the best stuff."

"Can you help us?" Ryart peered up at the nest. If Jewels could fly, she might be able to help him rescue Elphie.

"Well, I have a busy day of shopping ahead of me. First here, then to Eel Bay, then to the edges of the Amazon, then . . ."

"Please!" Ryart begged. "I can't climb trees, and my friend is up there. I think the crow grabbed her thinking she would make a nice decoration for his nest."

"Why would a crow think that?" the flying squirrel asked.

"Because," Ryart said exasperated, "she's a fixie."

"A fixie?" Jewels was confused.

"Half-fairy, half-pixie, 100 percent Wonderfolke. She's silver like the lining of a cloud. She was trying to fly," Ryart explained.

"A fixie! I've never met a fixie in person." Jewels exclaimed, clearly excited. "Say, what in the world is your friend doing . . . Hey, what's her name?"

"Elphie," Ryart said slowly. "Elphie Askul."

"What in the world is *Elphie Askul* doing here?" asked the flying squirrel, swirling her bracelet around at the dark expanse of trees.

"We were flying in Far Meadow," Ryart shared a little too quickly.

"Flying? Then why doesn't your friend just fly down here?" Jewels dropped her fists to her hips.

Ryart sat silent for a minute. He needed Jewels to help him, but he knew Elphie was not supposed to be flying quite yet. Reluctantly, he added, "Well . . . she's not supposed to fly quite yet. She's only ninety-nine and a quarter." Ryart lowered his eyes and kicked the dirt with his left paw. "Elphie was trying to teach herself."

Jewels stepped back, crossing her arms. She did not know a lot about the Wonderfolke, let alone fixies, but she knew as well as anyone that such an important rite of passage could not be rushed. Who did this young creature think she was, trying to take flight before it was time?

"Flying," Jewels snorted, "is a talent you have to *earn.*"

"Yes, yes. But she wanted to learn by her birthday so she could begin her life adventures as a full-fledged member of her troupe." He could have added more about how, as a fixie, Elphie was treated differently than the other youngsters in Homestead. She just wanted to fit in. But Ryart did not need to tell Jewels all of that; he just needed some help saving his friend before something awful happened.

This little hedgehog is in quite a pickle, Jewels thought. She had set aside the day to go shopping, but then again, she had an opportunity to meet a real-life fixie. Jewels had heard of them, of course—they had the prettiest clothing material—but to meet one, wow, what a treat! But she had places to be. Jewels rubbed her tummy with her right hand and patted her head with her left. After a few moments, she spoke, "Okay, I'll help. But one condition: your fixie friend has to tell me where she does her shopping. I've heard fixies are the snappiest of dressers."

"Deal!" Ryart said, not knowing what Jewels meant by that. As far as he knew, Elphie was the only fixie in Eludia. If Jewels had never met a fixie, how did she know they were snappy dressers? Ryart would worry about that later. For now, he had to get Elphie away from the crow.

♦

Elphie woke up in a strange place. The last thing she remembered was jumping off the rock. Between then and now was blank. Elphie realized quickly, though, she was in the heart of someone's nest. She was small enough to possibly squeeze through the side that towered above her. The tangle of twigs was dense, but not solid. *That could be tough,* she thought. *There must be another way out of this . . .*

Whipping her head anxiously around the nest, Elphie noticed bits and pieces of color—golds and silvers primarily—tucked in between the branches. Whoever owned this nest had decorated purposefully, if not messily.

It occurred to Elphie just then: the owner of the nest must have thought *she* was a decoration. Elphie had been confused for a tall fairy as well as a small pixie, but never a colorful scrap. *Oh, why do I have to be silver? If I was pink like my father or green like my mother, whoever owned this nest would have let me be, and I wouldn't be here.*

There was one particular bird that collected shiny objects in such a fashion, and when Elphie glimpsed a few stray black feathers in the massive nest, her throat went dry. *This is a crow's nest.*

Fairies and pixies did not get along with these large birds, and if the owner of this nest found out she was more than just a bright addition to its collection . . . she shivered.

Elphie scrambled to the top of the twigs and branches, gazed out, and saw the tops of trees. Only one was taller than where she found herself, a redwood. But when Elphie glanced down, she nearly caught her breath. She was higher than she had ever been before. Her heart beat faster, but it was not all fear; she was also *excited.*

This must be what it's like to fly, she thought excitedly. But it dawned on her; flying practice or not, this was too far for her first real flight. And unlike her climbs up and down Nahke, this was too dangerous. Elphie was stuck.

Just then, Elphie heard the crackle of a squawk. Without looking up, Elphie recognized the call right away: it was a crow, enemy of fairies and pixies. When Elphie sneaked a peek through the branches above the nest, her fears were confirmed. Perched on a heavy branch nearby was the biggest, baddest crow she'd ever seen. It peered out over the forest, sharp eyes searching for more decorations or something to eat.

"Oh, boy," she whispered quietly. "What am I going to do?"

Centuries ago, fairies and pixies had been friends with the crow. As flying creatures, they had a lot in common. But as more pixie folk moved to Eludia and built up their Homestead, the crows had been pushed out of their native habitat. When the butterflies stopped spreading the goodwill of the fairies and pixies, the crows struck back and initiated war. Elphie winced as she recalled the story her parents had told her when she was little.

Her mother Marri Golde remembered the crow wars. Elphie's fairy grandfather had passed in the conflict, as well as her pixie grandparents. The very first Crow King, Gigantor III, decreed any pixie or fairy found in Dark Forest or the surrounding area would have their wings plucked off. The lucky ones would be mercifully eaten. The unlucky ones would be released and forced to live the rest of their days without flying. Without the protection of their wings, their lives were doomed.

It was then the crow flapped his wings, jumping to the edge of the nest right above where Elphie was hidden.

The crow must not have realized I'm both pixie and fairy, she thought. *Otherwise, they would have plucked off my wings.*

Thinking fast, Elphie fell limply into the basin of the nest. Crows had good eyesight, but if she did not move, she might be able to continue to play the part of a scrap.

The bird dropped into the nest, making the entire structure vibrate under his taloned feet. She felt the smooth edge of the crow's beak poke at her. *Stay still,* Elphie told herself. It was a lesson her mother had taught her: when faced with danger, play dead. The crow poked her a little harder this time. He pecked at her blue dress. It hurt, but Elphie bravely stayed very still.

Seemingly convinced she was a scrap, the crow picked Elphie up and leapt to the edge of the nest. Dangling her over the side, Elphie could do nothing but hold her breath as the entire expanse of the Dark Forest wavered below her. Heights did not bother Elphie, but hanging helplessly hundreds of feet in the air made her stomach flip in nasty ways. She thought for sure that any moment the crow would lose interest and she would find herself plummeting to the shadowed ground below. Instead, the crow tilted its head to the side and tucked Elphie into the woven edge of the nest. It was not comfortable and she could no longer see the redwood. Elphie stayed limp to not alert the crow.

When the bird was satisfied with the placement of its new "ornament," it retreated back into the basin of the nest.

The crow does think I'm a decoration, Elphie thought with a sigh of relief before reconsidering her lot. *Now how am I going to escape?*

♦

"That's the plan?" Jewels tipped her head to the side with a bemused glint in her eyes. "You want me to fly up to a nest guarded by a crow, grab your friend who doesn't know me, then fly down here without being chased?"

Ryart thought for a moment. Maybe they did need a better plan.

"And . . . are you sure she's in that nest up there?" Jewels pointed to the only nest in the canopy of trees. Even more, it was the biggest, grandest, most ornamented nest in Dark Forest.

"Yes, the one with all the decorations," responded Ryart, gazing worriedly into the dead tree. "I'm sure Elphie's one of those shiny pieces way up there!"

"Hmm, uh-oh." Jewels carefully peered at the glittering ball of gold and silver in the pine. She suddenly groaned. "Oh boy. I recognize that nest now. That nest up there . . . that belongs to Condor, Kueen of the Crows."

"Queen? Do you mean Crow King?" Ryart asked.

"No – K-ueen. Like king and queen together. That's Condor, the Great They of They. Conder is the Crow Kueen."

"Oh, do you know them?" Ryart exclaimed, thrilled at the possibility of his friend being rescued. Jewels, with all her pizazz and pretty necklaces, seemed like the kind of squirrel who would know royalty.

"I know them all right," she answered dryly. "Condor is neither male nor female, just dominant energy. But I don't know them like you know Elphie. Condor has been Kueen the last few years, and within these trees, it's been a reign of terror. They have so many decorations up there because they take whatever they want. Condor grabs anything they can find that's gold or silver–living or not–and puts it on their nest. They have the best shopping, but even I'm not crazy enough to go near their nest. When I was flying through here last moon cycle, I heard Condor had de-winged a whole handful of Wonderfolke just for fun!"

The hedgehog's eyes went wide as he thought of the young fixie losing her bright silver wings that she had not even been able to use officially yet. "But we've got to save Elphie," Ryart said stubbornly, sitting on his haunches and putting his paws on his hips, gathering his courage. "I'm going to save my friend one way or the other, with or without your help. It would be great if you had a plan of your own; any ideas?"

Jewels rubbed her tummy with her right hand and patted her head with her left, her typical thinking position that helped her straighten out her thoughts. After a few moments, she spoke, "Okay, monsieur. Here's a new plan. How fast are you?"

"I'm super-fast," Ryart puffed his chest.

"Faster than a crow?"

"Definitely! I followed Condor to their nest at three-quarter speed."

Jewels chuckled, a chittering sound that echoed around them as she fluffed up her tail. "Let's see what you can do, then! Put this on." Jewels took off her golden necklace. The chain was thin, but it held a single, small golden acorn. Jewels removed the necklace and handed it to Ryart.

"Why?" asked Ryart as he gathered the shiny chain in his paws.

Jewels took a measured scan at the redwood, measuring the distance between it and the nest.

"I'm going to make my way to the top of that tree over there." Jewels pointed to the fat, thick-barked reddish tree that climbed to the sky higher than the rest. "It's close enough to Condor's home that I should be able to fly from it to the nest and find Elphie."

"Oh, what about Condor?" quizzed Ryart.

"That's where you come in. When you see me reach the top of the redwood, you come out of hiding, jump around like a chipmunk, then wave my necklace. Like this." Jewels waved her hands over her head, creating a new wave of shadows in the afternoon light that made it down to the forest floor. "It's big enough to catch Condor's attention. They'll see the jewelry and come for it. You run like the dickens, and I'll swoop into the nest and grab your friend. Try not to lose my necklace; my mama gave it to me when I first flew. Once you lose the Crow Kueen, we can meet up and you can properly introduce me to this rare fixie."

"Are you sure you want to use your necklace?" asked a bewildered Ryart. He had only just met this unique flying squirrel, and he was awed at how helpful she'd turned out to be. Squirrels were notorious for being all over the place, whether they could fly or not.

"Yes," replied Jewels, and for a moment her face got very serious when she glanced at Ryart. "Condor took all my jewelry once and wouldn't give it back. Everything I worked so hard to collect is sitting up there in their big home except this special necklace. If I can help you, that'll make me and Condor square."

"Sounds good! Why don't we meet up at Deep Creek, then? At the point where it's narrowest? That should be far enough that the Crow Kueen won't worry about us anymore."

"Sounds good." Jewels took a deep breath. "Okay, cover me. I'm going for the redwood. We just have to hope Condor doesn't see me before I reach the top."

◆

The thrill of being up so high was starting to wear off, and the sharp branches poking into Elphie's spine were starting to really hurt. She was not sure what she was going to do, but she knew she could not stay way up here much longer. Out of the corner of her eye, through a few tangled chunks of her hair, she could see the orange sun falling lazily behind the horizon. If she was not home by dark, not only would she be vulnerable to all the creatures who hunted at night, her parents would possibly ground her from flying at all. But if the crow found out she was a fixie, she'd lose her wings for sure, and for longer than one hundred years.

Just then she felt a rubbing on her leg. *What was that?*

Elphie looked down and noticed the second grub trying to get out of her satchel. Luckily, her bag was made by Wonderfolke so nothing could escape. But seeing the little creature trying to wriggle its way out of the magical fabric gave her an idea.

That's it! I can distract the crow with the grub.

Elphie craned her neck cautiously over the side of the nest and surveyed the pine tree's dead branches beneath her. Maybe, if she timed it just right and the wind did not pick up, she might be close enough to jump from one bough down to the next after setting the grub free as a distraction. As her heart pounded, she did her best to focus and thought of what she could do, step-by-step.

If I go slow, she thought, *I should be able to control my drop by going branch to branch. If I can make it safely to the ground, I can make it back to the big rock in Far Meadow. If I can make it to the big rock, I can meet up with Ryart and we can zoom back home. Then everything will be fine, but how do I know when to go for it?*

Elphie just needed to wait for the right time. She needed a sign.

◆

Meanwhile, Jewels dashed from the bushes to the base of the redwood, crunching layers of the underbrush beneath her feet. She was not fast on the ground, but she could not fly until she was high up. Ryart carefully watched the crow, keeping one eye on his new friend making a slow dash between the trees.

Jewels was nearly to the tree when Condor jumped to the top of the tangle of branches and peered out over the woods. They were on the opposite side from the redwood, but Ryart knew that Jewel's and his plan was already in trouble: with their incredible eyesight, it would only be a matter of time before Condor spotted Jewels. If the Crow Kueen saw the flying squirrel on the ground, she would be a goner.

Without thinking, Ryart broke lightning fast for Jewels. Condor hopped around the edge of their nest, coming around to the side by the redwood. Ryart accelerated, tackling Jewels and dragging her behind the towering tree, just in the nick of time.

"What was that?" Jewels whispered harshly.

Ryart covered her mouth and pointed up toward the nest. Jewels glanced around the redwood and saw the crow surveying the forest on their side of the crow's nest. She had almost been spotted.

"Thank you," Jewels mouthed. She did not know very many hedgehogs, but this one was really brave. She was glad to have made a new friend. When her nerves settled, Jewels began to climb, keeping the tree between her and Condor.

◆

Elphie knew that when the crow moved to the far side of the nest, it was time. Slowly, she pulled the grub out of her satchel, then squeezed her way through the branches until she reached the inside of the nest. If she had been a full-size pixie, she would never have fit. This was one of the few times she was grateful to be different.

Finally, she had squirmed through enough to reach a gap in the twigs. She dropped the grub into the basin of the crow's home and watched it plop on the floor. Her distraction was set. Elphie worked her way back to the outside of the nest. All she needed now was for the crow to spot the grub so she could escape undetected.

The crow's head cocked but their attention was on something below the redwood, not the grub. Frowning with frustration, Elphie decided to take the time to plot her path down from what felt like the top of the world.

The first drop was only a few feet, so she felt comfortable she could make that. From there she pictured the rest of her precarious descent down the tree, branch by thin branch. She could not quite see how far the last drop would be to the ground, but Elphie was not ready to worry about that just yet. If she could just make it to the last branches, she would have a good chance at making it back home alive. She steeled herself for the descent.

Suddenly, Elphie heard the crow jump down into the basin of the nest. *This is it!* she thought. *The crow will eat the grub, and most importantly, won't be able to see me.*

Elphie took a deep breath, stretched her young wings, and jumped for the first branch.

◆

Jewels reached the top of the redwood just as Condor jumped into the nest. Then she saw a flurry of silver drop into the dead branches. Back down on the forest floor, Ryart leapt out from behind the tree like a crazed chipmunk, waving the gold necklace. Jewels readied herself, legs curled under her on her branch, ready to launch. She kept her eyes on Condor to see if they would take the bait.

Wait just a minute, Jewels thought, her black eyes narrowing. That silver falling from the Crow Kueen's nest was actually moving on its own. It was the fixie! A real, honest-to-goodness, fixie. She was not flying but jumping from branch to branch.

Holy Jupiter! That must be Elphie. She's escaping!

Jewels smirked, proud of the little creature for planning her own way out of the crow's nest, but . . . oh no. It dawned on her that Condor was safely in their nest and could not see below. Elphie could probably make it, but now Ryart was making all sorts of noise.

"Ryart!" she whispered as loudly as she could. "Ryart, stop making noise!"

But she was too far away, and the hedgehog was persistent. Just then, Condor jumped to the top of their nest. When the Crow Kueen saw the gold being waved around by the hedgehog, Condor spread their wings and flapped them wildly.

"No one bothers my friend! Go away, you Featherhead!" Jewels heard Ryart scream at the top of his lungs.

Condor swooped down toward the little hedgehog. Jewels watched helplessly until she saw Ryart turn and run. *Wow,* she thought, *he* is *fast!* But was he fast enough? She had to trust that he was.

Jewels turned her attention back to the dead pine and watched as Elphie picked her way down the tree. *No pixie is that agile,* thought Jewels. *No fairy is that graceful. She glides from branch to branch, no matter how big or small the next one is.*

But then Jewels traced Elphie's path with her eyes. Her heart hammered when she saw how big the drop from the last set of branches was. It was too far for most creatures, but especially for a Wonderfolke who was not yet one hundred years old. She would have to save Elphie.

Jewels took flight.

◆

Elphie planted her feet on the rough bark of each branch as she dropped, training her gaze on the next fall below her. When she reached the last set of branches, Elphie froze. That drop had to be ten times higher than she'd ever flown in Far Meadows. But she was not about to let fear stop her now. She wanted to learn to fly, so, without thinking, Elphie jumped.

She pumped her wings as hard as she could, but the ground was coming up fast. She thought of her father and mother and Nahke, closed her eyes, and braced for impact.

Just a daisy-stem length away from the ground, something furry and soft collided with Elphie. The smell of green apples enveloped her. The creature held her tight, and they barrel-rolled across the earth. When they came to a stop, the creature was lying on her back and Elphie sat on top. The creature opened up her arms and let Elphie go free.

Elphie got up slowly, brushed herself off, straightened her dress, and assessed her rescuer. She appeared to be a squirrel, but she did not think squirrels could fly.

"Bonjour," said the squirrel, smiling broadly.

"Wow, thank you," stammered Elphie. "Who are you? What are you?"

"Moi? Why, I am the Magnificent Flying Frances. I am a flying squirrel. You can call me Jewels," she said with a wink. "I'm friends with Ryart. We came to rescue you."

"Oh, Ryart!" Elphie searched around desperately. "Where is Ryart?"

"It's okay, Elphie. He's fast."

"Super-fast," added the fixie.

"Yes, super-fast. In the meantime," Jewels looked up and around, "we have to get out of here before Condor comes back."

Elphie raised her eyebrows. "Who's Condor?" This flying squirrel could not mean who she thought she meant.

"The Kueen of the Crows. They're the one who captured you."

Elphie's jaw dropped. Of all the crows, she had been captured by the Crow Kueen.

"C'mon," Jewels insisted. "No time to just stand there. We have to head to Deep Creek. We'll meet Ryart at the narrowest point. Can you move?"

Elphie nodded. She was still pretty stunned from how close she'd gotten to hitting the hard ground, but surprisingly she was not hurt. Flexing her wings gratefully, she gave Jewels a confident smile.

"Okay, let's get out of here." Jewels scanned Elphie up and down. "By the way, I love your blue dress. You'll have to tell me where you shop."

Elphie grinned and the two headed for Deep Creek.

◆

Elphie and Jewels sat on the shallow edge of the creek and waited. As the sun got lower, the lighting and sounds of the woods around them began to change. Night was almost here, and with it came different creatures and dangers that Elphie had only heard about. As the water bubbled by, she anxiously watched sparrows flying back to their homes and bugs skittering into their holes. Glancing at Jewels, she saw worry in her new friend's eyes as well. It felt like Ryart had been gone forever.

Finally, Elphie heard a rustle in the underbrush and sprang to her feet. Ryart approached them, and when he got close, he stood with his paws behind his back. The hedgehog seemed utterly exhausted.

"Ryart!" exclaimed Elphie and Jewels at the same time. The two rushed toward the little hedgehog and hugged him. "You did it!"

"*We* did it," said Ryart. "We couldn't have done it without each other. Elphie, I'm so glad you made it out of there safely! Are you hurt? Isn't it amazing that Jewels can fly? All I did was just run as fast as I always do."

Elphie chuckled, but then she saw a disappointed look on Jewels' face. The flying squirrel was moving her eyes up and down the hedgehog, as if he was missing something.

"Oh, it looks like you had to drop the necklace to save yourself," Jewels mumbled.

"Well . . ." Ryart began slowly.

Jewels' head sank against her chest. "It's okay. I'm just glad you're okay."

Ryart pulled his paws from behind his back, revealing the glittering gold necklace. "Your mom's gift is safe with me."

Jewels' face lit up. "Oh, Ryart!" she said, engulfing the hedgehog.

"No one, and I mean no one, can catch me," Ryart said with a grin.

"Jewels," Elphie said warmly. "It was nice meeting you, but I've got to get back home before dark. I hope we meet again."

"It was a pleasure to meet you both." Jewels bowed graciously. "It's not 'good-bye,' it's 'see you soon.' I think we will be friends for a long time to come."

The three smiled and embraced.

"Ryart, do you have one more run in you? Can you get us home before dark?" asked the fixie.

"For you, Elphie, always. Climb on." The two waved to Jewels, then zoomed home to the fixie's troupe.

◆

The summer sun was just setting to the west when Elphie and Ryart arrived on the outskirts of Milkweed Fields. Elphie hugged the hedgehog, then ran home to Nahke as fast as she could, eager to tell her mother about her day. When she got to the base of the tree, she could smell Marri Golde's cooking and hear the familiar sounds of the family home. Her mother was preparing one of Elphie's favorites: dandelion blossoms with a side of rose petal. Her father was in the bottom hollow preparing for tomorrow's work on the farm. Elphie was home.

"How was your day, Love?" Marri Golde asked when Elphie climbed into Nahke. Elphie lit up when retelling about her day, minus the flying part in Far Meadow. The young fixie skipped over those details by focusing on the escape, and brushing over the part that might get her into a little bit of trouble.

Marri Golde listened as Elphie recounted her adventures. Her daughter certainly showed courage by facing Condor and escaping without help from other Wonderfolke. Perhaps the young fixie did have the right combination of courage, empathy, and teamwork needed to teach majesty properly to the Monarch Queen during the Emergence.

"It was different, Mama," Elphie said with a smile as she wrapped up her stories about her adventures in Dark Forest. "But sometimes, different is good."

The Bulli Badger

Elphie Askul hated grumps. Six moon cycles from today, Elphie turned one hundred. But today, those six moon cycles felt like six hundred. For eons, her father Po partnered with the titan beetles to do some of the heavy lifting around the farm. However, her family's prized titan beetle, Alice, was being stubborn and did not want her pincers washed.

The farm was her father's domain and Elphie sometimes wondered if that's all her father cared about. Elphie's mother had the Emergence and Nahke took care of the schooling and the home, but it was her father who loved to play in the Eludian dirt. Po liked coming home with dirty hands and dusty clothes. Elphie thought it reminded him of being a young pixie growing up in Homestead.

The pixie's little patch of peace was planted at the bottom of Nahke's hill, on the eastern boundaries of Milkweed Fields. Her father chose the spot to ensure his garden received the "freshest" rays of sunlight each morning. It was a lesson Po had learned from his mother. She had cared deeply for all living things. Po used the land to augment the acorns Nahke provided.

In addition to the sustenance the farm offered, Po had two spots that he tended to with extra love and care. Elphie had overheard Po tell Nahke once that those were his favorite places in all of Eludia.

The first was the field of flowers. The field was filled with reds, greens, blues, and Mare's favorite: purples–deep hues and light lavenders. Each evening, Po would fly with Marri Golde to the flower patch and the two would stroll through the long rows of colors, the tips of their wings holding on to one another's. They had a love borne of understanding and molded by six hundred years of togetherness. Those moments in the garden were for her father and mother alone.

Po's other favorite spot was the grub farm, which consisted of titan beetle offspring. The pixie protected the descendants of his titan beetle friend, Alice. Titans were the largest-known beetle in Eludia. They were solitary creatures who avoid conflict, but if called into battle, these 'gentle giants' became courageous warriors. They defended themselves against predators by using their sharp spines and strong jaws. The powerful insects were as long as the tallest pixies and a similar shade of color to Elphie's eyes. Their mandibles could snap a pixie in two and a fairy lengthwise, if they wanted. Thankfully, the titan beetles and Wonderfolke were friends.

Po had been close to Alice's family since he and Marri Golde first came to Milkweed Fields. Back then, titans were independent sorts who rarely interacted with anyone. But a few hundred years ago, the number of titan beetles began to dwindle. The titans became rare, not because they were weak, they were slow to anger, but amongst the fiercest warriors. Their numbers shrank because in all of Eludia, titan beetle grubs were the most delicious.

The grub of a titan was a prize in Eludia. It has a savory creaminess that was undeniable. Bears, crows, Hoo birds, and badgers all loved to eat grubs. So did most other creatures. But of all the grubs to eat, the titan grub was the grandest. The titans fought fervently for generations to protect their larvae, but to no avail; nearly everyone was eaten.

The summer after Marri Golde was invited back to perform the Emergence by the Grand Troupe Council, Alice's great-great-grandmother (to the 331st degree) struck a deal with Po: in exchange for safe care of her offspring, the titans would give the pixie all but three of her larvae for Po's grub farm. The pixie would then protect those three larvae with the full extent of his ability. The other larvae–the grubs–would be raised in a separate part of the farm. Before these grubs reached maturity, Po would trade the plumpest with Eludian creatures for information or favors.

The cost was steep for the beetles, but the titans had weighed their options carefully before striking the bargain with the pixie. Alice's descendants figured it was a deal with Po or face extinction. For the guaranteed survival of their species, the titans found the deal to be bearable.

Soon after Po had struck the deal with Alice's ancestors, the partnership between pixie and titan beetle spread throughout Homestead. During the Emergence, the other pixie troupes witnessed Po's titan beetle carrying a huge batch of chrysalis. The beasts were good workers, but hard to find.

The work was beneficial, but it was Po's deal for grubs that really enticed the Wonderfolke. To the pixies in Homestead, taking care of three titan beetle larvae per year seemed like a great trade for access to dozens of the tastiest grubs in all of Eludia.

The pixies certainly saw value in the agreement, but so did the beetles. Where other titan families became fewer and fewer, Alice's lineage continued to stay strong. So strong that each generation of titan beetle renewed the agreement with Po until it was believed to be true.

What was different about Po's relationship with his titan friends was that the pixie gave a piece of his wing to one beetle per generation. Alice was amongst a long line of titan beetles who had received the gift.

Po's relationship with the titans was one of mutual respect and trust. With Alice, she and Po bonded completely. Their work ethics were equally impressive and though titans did not speak and pixies could not talk "insect," the two were closer than even the intimacy of native tongues. It was a relationship rooted by a generational family tree, nurtured by long days in the sun, working the farm in silence.

Po had come to know the secrets of the titan beetles, but he never used the information against the insects. Instead, Po used the knowledge to understand the beetles for more than a way to clear flowers and mushrooms, pull large loads of rocks and twigs, and work the Milkweed Fields after the Emergence. Po saw Alice—and each of her ancestors—as individuals.

Now that those in Homestead had made the same arrangement with their own titan beetle families, every aspect of a titan's larvae-hood was the same across Eludia. The only exception was the gifting; no Wonderfolke had ever done that before. But for all titan beetles, the offspring would spend their larvae-hood in Eludia, most likely on a pixie grub farm just like

Po's. Upon maturity, the larvae would set off on an Outside Experience, or their "O.E." Their O.E. started at the end of adolescence with the giant beetles leaving their farms and traveling to the Weeping Tree. Most creatures never traveled to the Weeping Tree, but the titans were a unique breed. They were not just big, they did big things.

Few titans made it to the Weeping Tree. But those who did returned to their host pixie family and stayed loyal to the same troupe that raised them. The now-older titans would never speak of their Outside Experience.

Alice had traveled on her O.E. years before. She had left one morning as a barely transformed larvae and returned to Elphie's troupe as a six-and-a-half inchworm giantess.

True to form, as exotic as her trip must have been, Alice had never spoken of it. The titan beetle had just showed up one morning, ready to work. Elphie remembered Po smiling when he saw her, but no words were exchanged. They just enjoyed working together in silence.

But this morning, Alice was being difficult. Elphie sometimes wondered if the titan beetle purposely dug-in with the fixie because the beetle wanted to work with Elphie's father. But the fixie put that thought aside. One day she would take over responsibility for the farm; she needed to have a relationship with the titans herself.

It was just right now, Alice was being a pain. Elphie needed to find a resolution.

◆

Each morning before the sun was up, Elphie's troupe sat down to a big breakfast. The kitchen hollow faced the East so the early morning light crawled into their home and warmed Nahke. The light revealed a meal of wildflowers, mushrooms, and–if they were lucky–honey. The morning meal appeared as if by magic, but Elphie knew her father was responsible for the first meal of the day.

Whenever the troupe had honeycombs, Elphie would sneak one back to her private hollow where she would wrap the comb in rose petals. The gift would be presented to Alice as they started their first-light chores (and before Papa checked on them).

Elphie's last chore was always to wash Alice. The fixie would walk Alice to the edge of where the fields bordered the wood and where the ground was thick with carpet moss, and then try to cajole the stubborn creature into letting her wash her down.

Alice would have nothing of it. She hated being washed.

"C'mon now, Alice," Elphie whispered, taking off her satchel and laying it near an acorn shell full of water. "Papa would never let you go back into the woods looking as if you've worked hard all morning. Let me tidy you up." The beetle turned away from the fixie.

The sun was approaching midday and the young fixie desperately wanted to meet Ryart and Jewels. The three were going to a favorite watering hole, Freedo's Pond, to listen to bullfrogs and lounge on lily pads.

Alice, however, was being difficult. She just would not stay still. Pixies could talk to mammals, birds, and fish; fairies could talk to reptiles, amphibians, and insects. Elphie was a fixie–half-fairy, half-pixie–so she could chat with anyone in Eludia. Titans did not speak much, but Elphie had figured out titans understood the native language of beetles, even if they did not speak it. The intimacy of using Beetleoid usually coaxed Alice into action. Today, however, the stubborn insect was not communicating.

"C'mon Alice," Elphie clicked, putting her sponge into the acorn shell that held a few dewdrops of water. "Let me wash your pincers. I'm supposed to meet my friends soon."

Alice maneuvered to keep her rear end between the fixie and the beetle's mouth. Each time Elphie came close, Alice rotated. The fixie chased the beetle round and round, eventually knocking over the acorn shell and nearly drenching her satchel. The fixie collapsed on the carpet moss, exhausted.

But sitting on the ground gave her a new perspective. Elphie noticed something was wrong with Alice's left pincer; there was a slight cut midway up the side of her mandible.

"Oh, Alice. What happened?" Elphie got to her feet with her hands out-stretched. "It's okay, I'm not going to hurt you. Let me see what I can do."

Alice relented and let the young fixie assess her pincer. It was only a small cut, but it seemed irritated. Elphie scooped up a little moss and whispered a couple words over it.

"Alice, this is going to sting a little, but it'll make you feel better. I'm going to put it on your pincer." Alice watched Elphie cautiously, keeping three of her four eyes trained on her escape route.

"It'll be okay, I promise Alice," Elphie clicked. All four eyes came around and the titan beetle squatted still. Elphie applied the medicine to the cut. "There, that should feel better in a little bit."

Alice nuzzled Elphie before scuttling into the wood. The fixie watched the beetle go, then looked down at her shadow. It was almost gone, meaning it was nearly time to meet Ryart. He would be waiting. Jewels was going to meet them at the pond.

Done with her chores, Elphie put the acorn shell away and picked up her satchel. She went to find her father who was on the farm's northern boundary updating their stone fence. Po was replacing smaller pebbles with two-handers–rocks light enough to lift, but not just with one hand. Her father always worked alone when he wasn't with Alice.

"Papa, do you mind if I take a mushroom stem and three grubs today? Ryart, Jewels, and I are headed to Freedo's Pond." Elphie always took two grubs for Ryart and one for Jewels. The stem was for herself.

"What time will you be home, Love?" Po gazed into Elphie's ginger-bread eyes.

"I'll be home by dark, Papa. I promise."

"Did you let your mother know?" Po asked sternly.

"I will, Papa," offered Elphie.

"And you washed Alice?" questioned her father.

"Yes, Papa. Alice was a little grumpy, but I took care of her." The fixie smiled.

"Okay, then," Po rustled his daughter's hair. "Pick out a good stem and take three grubs with you. Make sure you close the gate to the grub farm this time. I don't want to draw the attention of any crows."

"Okay, Papa. I'll be home by dark." Elphie kissed her father.

"Before you go, can you give your mama a kiss from me and this?" Po reached over a low point in the stone wall and picked up a single flower. He twirled the blue-purple lobelia before handing the bloom to Elphie. "This is your mother's favorite. I found a patch this morning. I'll be transplanting the patch to the field I'm developing for your mother."

"Of course, Papa," Elphie didn't understand her mother and father's love. He was always in the fields and her mother was always studying ritual. They did, however, do nice things for one another.

Elphie put the thought aside and took the rich blue-purple flower and inhaled deeply, smiling at her father. Elphie stood on her toes and kissed her father on the cheek. "I'll give it to her straightaway."

A short while later, the young fixie found her mother in the garden. Her mother was moving from one plot to another, whispering to rosemary.

"Mama, this is for you, from Papa." Elphie extended the bloom.

"Oh, Elphie! Thank you. Your father knows my favorite." The fairy breathed in the flower's beauty. "I can mix this with my afternoon tea. Thank you, my love."

"Mama, do you need anything before I meet Ryart and Jewels?"

"No, Love, but thank you for asking. What trouble are you three getting into today? Not flying, I hope."

"No flying, I promise," responded Elphie swaying from side to side.

"You know you have to wait until you're one hundred to fly. You're still six moon cycles short," Marri Golde cautioned.

"Yes, Mama. No flying."

Marri Golde's aqua blue eyes searched Elphie carefully. Finally, the fixie became still.

"Okay, then you have fun. Be home by dark," the fairy smiled.

Elphie kissed her mother, then rushed to the garden glad that her real day was about to begin. She picked a medium-sized mushroom stem from the cluster in the corner, then ran to the grub farm and selected the three plumpest ones, putting them into her satchel. Elphie buckled her bag and set off as quickly as she could for the outskirts of Milkweed Fields. Sure enough, the little hedgehog was waiting for her.

"Ready to zoom, Elphie?" Ryart smiled.

"Ready, Ryart!" Elphie climbed on Ryart's back and the two set off.

◆

"Is this a shortcut, Ryart?" Elphie asked after a little while. They'd gone on adventures to the nearby pond to swim in the waters and hunt for shiny rocks many times, but the groves of trees they were zooming past seemed different.

"Oh yes!" Ryart called proudly over his shoulder. "I know all the fastest paths around here. I found this one the other day."

Elphie laughed. "I didn't know we'd be headed this way, but I'm pretty sure the willder bees live nearby!"

"Willder bees? Those sound dangerous."

"Oh, not at all! They are peaceful farmers. Fairies and pixies trade nectar with the willder bees for their honey. Everyone thinks the bees are mean, but they actually make the best combs in all of Eludia."

"Honeycombs? I *love* honeycombs!" exclaimed her friend.

"Who doesn't, Ryart? And your shortcut takes us right by their hive." Elphie paused. "Let's stop in and see if they'll share any."

"Sounds great!" squealed the hedgehog.

Moments later, Ryart and Elphie pulled up to an ancient elm tree that climbed to the sky and sprawled across the forest floor. Bees swarmed around the tree's gaping hole, and their low-pitched warbling echoed down to Elphie's ears. She was about to say something to Ryart about the last time she'd visited here, but her eyebrows narrowed, and she frowned. There were bits of honey smeared all around the opening to the hive. Something seemed out of place. The bees would not be so disorganized to leave a mess like that out for all to see.

Before Elphie or Ryart could figure out what had happened, one of the queen's guards rushed up. He was as angry as a hornet.

"Trezpazers! Trezpazers! You muzt leave at once," stated the bee in Eludian, brandishing his stinger.

Ryart cowered backward a few steps, and Elphie could feel him shaking from where she sat on his back. But she straightened her own shoulders and put up a hand in greeting. "Mizter Willder Bee," said Elphie in perfect Honeybee. "What happened here?"

Upon hearing the fixie fluently speak his language, the soldier calmed down.

"We were attacked by Mortimer yezterday. That big bear comez by the hive every mid-afternoon and takez mozt of our honey."

Elphie gasped and Ryart gave her a worried look, not understanding the bee's language. Bears were not friendly to anyone in the forest, and Elphie knew better than to be anywhere near where they lived in Eludia. "I'm zo zorry," replied Elphie. "Iz everyone okay?"

"Yez, but hiz fur iz too thick for our ztingerz. We were able to move Queen Zima and her baby beez higher up in the tree to protect them, but we can't ztop him."

"I'm glad everyone iz okay, Mizter Bee. We were juzt on our way to Freedo'z Pond and thought we'd ztop by for zome combz." Elphie knew at that point, however, that these creatures were much too busy preparing for another potential attack from Mortimer to worry about sharing any delicious honeycombs with her and Ryart, but still she hoped.

"Wonderfolke are alwayz welcome here. I'll tell the queen you were here." The soldier bowed at the abdomen, ignoring Elphie's comments about honeycombs. "By the way, be careful at the pond. Our lookoutz told uz a mean badger waz prowling around there."

"Thank you, Mizter Bee. We'll be careful." Elphie peered at Ryart, who had not understood a word of the conversation she had just had since it had been in Honeybee. *What he doesn't know won't hurt him,* she thought. Freedo's Pond was rumored to have the best lily pad lounging and the fixie wanted to get some late fall sun. "We'll let you get back to your work and will be on our way. Good luck with the clean-up."

The soldier bee disappeared back into the swarm.

"So, what happened?" asked Ryart.

"Mortimer the bear keeps taking their honey," translated Elphie. Ryart seemed concerned. "They were able to protect the queen from his latest attack though. These willder bees are a brave lot. But I don't think we'll be getting any honeycomb today. C'mon, we can still meet Jewels and have most of the day at the pond. You ready?"

The hedgehog nodded slowly at first, then his head picked up speed. Finally, his face broke into a giant smile.

"Let's zoom, Elphie!"

In no time, the two arrived at the south end of Freedo's Pond. The water smelled like coconut and was surrounded by trees covered in cocos vines, native to this part of Eludia. The vines wrapped themselves around the longstanding trees, sapping enough energy to keep the canopy sparse. This ensured the pond was always bathed in afternoon sun.

Pussy willows and long grass marched right up to the edge of the shore everywhere except for where they stood. Here, there was a little dirt ramp that led to the water. Lily pads were sprinkled across the pond like freckles, and Elphie's heart leapt with excitement as Ryart skidded to a halt. This would be the perfect, peaceful place to spend her afternoon with her friends.

"We're here!" exclaimed Ryart. Elphie jumped down and took off her satchel, laying it on the shore. Ryart gazed in awe at the tranquil bank before them. "It's so peaceful here."

Just then, an unidentified flying object swooped in over their heads. Ryart ducked, but Elphie giggled.

"Jewels! You made it!" the fixie squealed, thrilled that her "friend-troupe" was together again. A friend-troupe was different than the troupe a fairy or pixie was born into, or their familial troupe. Elphie, Jewels, and Ryart had become very close. Yes, the two Eludian creatures were not Wonderfolke, but she was as close with the flying squirrel and hedgehog as she was with anyone else in all of Eludia. Ryart was like a kid brother to her. Jewels, like a close sister. And since she had no siblings, the two of them had become her troupe.

"Moi? *Of course*, I made it. Wouldn't miss it." The flying squirrel landed effortlessly, wearing a gold necklace and a shiny new ankle bracelet.

"Like it?" Jewels stuck out her foot and waved around the anklet. "I went to the distant shores of the Blue Nile."

"I don't like it, Jewels . . . I *love* it," Elphie grinned. Ryart rolled his eyes.

The three threw themselves down near the water and dove into conversation. It had been a little while since they'd seen each other last. Finally, the talking slowed, and they settled into the comfort of quiet. After a while, Jewels spoke,

"Well, I'm climbing the tallest tree on the north side of the water so I can chase some dragonflies. Want to join me, Elphie?"

Elphie set her sights on the massive tree across the serene pond, then cringed. "I think we all know what happened the last time I tried to fly." The three giggled. "I'm going to grab a lily pad and float out to the middle of the pond to catch some rays. What about you, Ryart?"

"Me?" asked the hedgehog. "I'm going to sit right here on the shore."

"Sounds good. Shall we meet in an hour for a snack?" The three agreed.

◆

Elphie lounged on a pad floating freely just offshore. Dragonflies danced in the skies while bullfrogs filled the air with music. Jewels climbed trees and playfully dive-bombed unsuspecting insects on the north side of the water. Elphie sat up on her elbows, shielding her eyes and peering over at her hedgehog friend.

"Ryart," Elphie called impatiently, "come play in the pond!"

The prickly animal lay on his back on the sandy shore, all four paws stuck straight up in the air. "Elphie," Ryart responded jokingly in an Eludian dialect tinted with a hint of shrew, "I don't want to. I am perfectly content right here."

The hedgehog unexpectedly squeezed out a long, whistling fart.

"What was that?" Elphie asked, giggling.

"My butt sneezed," responded Ryart. The two laughed.

"Suit yourself." Elphie playfully plugged her nose for a moment before grasping the pad and buzzing her wings, urging the pad toward the center of the water. She was not sure why Ryart did not want to enjoy the pond with her, since he was usually more playful. Was he still worried about the willder bees after encountering their damaged hive on the way here? She was not sure. Before she was out of earshot, she looked back at her friend and cried out, "Oh, if you're interested, there's a big, fat grub in my satchel. I picked it out for you this morning. Only take one." That would definitely cheer him up.

Ryart's eyes lit up and he clapped all four paws together, rolling over to his tummy. He hurried over to Elphie's bag. The Wonderfolke had made the satchel, so there was a hidden trick to opening it. But Elphie had taught him how last spring.

Ryart glimpsed over his shoulder to thank the fixie, but she was nearly to the center of the water and would not hear him. He turned back to the bag, but before he could open the satchel, a deep voice boomed from the wood:

"Give me your lunch."

Ryart leapt back from Elphie's bag. *What in the world?* he thought, peering at the bag. A giant badger pushed his way through the brush in front of Ryart and onto the shore.

"Game over, dirtball; give me your grubs," the creature demanded in a harsh Eludian dialect.

"Who are you?" Ryart asked, surprised. He'd never encountered a badger before, but the way he towered over Ryart made the hedgehog tremble in fear.

"I'm Bulli the Badger. If you're going to hang out at the pond, you gotta give me whatever you got in the bag."

Ryart knew Elphie and Jewels were too far away to help. He would have to take care of this himself. There was no way he was going to hand over the delicious food Elphie had brought for them . . . at least not without a fight.

◆

Elphie enjoyed the quiet. It was rare she had time all to herself. The frogs sang on the shore, but out here, everything was so peaceful. The occasional insect buzzed by to say hello, but otherwise it was just her, blue sky, and the late fall sun. She sighed, glad to have a break from the hectic tasks she had to complete on the family farm and all the schooling she'd done to learn ritual and languages. Part of her really wanted to join Jewels up in the towering tree and give her wings another shot at flying, but today was supposed to be relaxing. Just then, an ancient dragonfly landed on her lily pad.

"Well, hello Mister Dragonfly," Elphie said with the utmost respect. "What brings you by?"

"A badger." The ancient flier twitched his wings. "A tree he put your friend in."

Elphie shot up straight and stared at the shore. Sure enough, it seemed as if Ryart was dangling upside down with a vine tied around his back paws. A large badger sat beneath him, fumbling with what looked like her bag. The dragonfly zipped away to the north.

Oh no! He's in trouble again. I have to get back to shore, Elphie thought. *And fast.*

She searched for Jewels, but the squirrel was nowhere to be found. Elphie glanced desperately around the pond in case anyone else would be able to see her if she took flight. Everything was quiet, so she chose to take the risk. Without hesitation, she clenched her eyes, leapt up in the air, fluttered her wings, and headed toward her friend as quickly as she could. Elphie had to protect her friend-troupe.

◆

"Let me down!" screeched Ryart.

The badger ignored the hedgehog and instead fumbled with the satchel. Bulli's paws were too big to open the small bag. He could feel the yumminess squirming around inside, but he could not get them out. His stomach moaned. Bulli shook the bag over his head, but again, nothing fell out.

"How do you open this bag?" the badger finally shouted at the hedgehog, annoyed.

"I'll never show you!" Ryart called out defiantly.

"Harumph," snorted Bulli as he turned the satchel over and over in his paws. "Then you'll stay up in that tree forever."

Just then, Elphie landed on shore. It was not the most graceful of landings, but she only stumbled for a moment before catching her balance not far from where the badger was tearing at her satchel. Bulli put the bag in his lap and smiled menacingly at the young Wonderfolke, his head titled quizzically.

"What do you want, Grasshopper?" the badger snarled.

"I'm here for my friend," Elphie responded, placing her hands on her hips and jerking her chin up toward Ryart.

"The hedgehog?" The badger licked his lips, lifted his left eyebrow, and admired the tiny morsel hanging by his back paws. "I'm saving him for dinner."

Elphie gasped, but Ryart swung punches defiantly in the air.

"You won't have me without a fight, Bulli!" Ryart yelled.

"Quiet down," Bulli said, flicking the hedgehog and sending him spinning in circles. Anger sparked in Elphie's heart and her jaw tightened with frustration. What could she do to get her friend down without being snatched up by the long-taloned badger herself?

Suddenly, Jewels swooped in at lightning speed. She went straight for Ryart, missing him by a hair. Caught off guard by her first attempt to rescue her friend, Bulli readied himself for Jewels' return flight. On her second approach, Bulli effortlessly swatted the squirrel out of the air. She landed hard at the base of a nearby tree. Before Jewels could steady herself, Bulli was on the flying squirrel, a vine quickly wrapped around her hind paws. Moments later, Jewels was hanging upside down beside Ryart.

Elphie watched the whole thing happen in seconds. Fear began to bubble in her gut. She was so stunned at how quickly it had all taken place that she had no time to help. Bulli turned back to the fixie, a nasty look of triumph in his dark eyes.

"Now you're going to join your friends, Grasshopper."

Elphie steadied herself. She had to think of something. And fast. But before she could, she was hanging upside down with her friend-troupe.

Once they were taken care of, Bulli continued to fumble with the bag while Elphie, Ryart, and Jewels watched. The badger mumbled to himself, and his stomach answered on more than one occasion. If the satchel had not been made by Wonderfolke, it would have been torn to shreds long ago by the powerful badger. As it was, the bag kept the prizes safe.

"Dagnabit! I can smell the grubs, but I can't get to them." Bulli's tummy rumbled even louder. Elphie felt her throat go dry when she noticed how hungry the big, dangerous creature was. With each passing second, she got more concerned that the badger would drop her enchanted bag and decide to quiet his stomach with her and her friends.

But suspended upside down, Elphie had a new perspective: *Since we obviously can't fight out way out of this, maybe there's another way we can avoid being eaten this afternoon.*

"Mister Badger–Mister Bulli–I can open the bag for you," Elphie offered calmly.

The large creature paused. "Harumph. Why would you do that? So I don't eat you instead?"

Elphie felt her friends' gaze on her, no doubt wondering what she was up to. She steadied herself, then continued. "Mister Bulli, I can hear your stomach talking from here. I'm happy to give you my grubs." The badger peered at her suspiciously as Elphie continued, "My parents gave me a big breakfast. It sounds like you haven't eaten in a while."

"Well . . ." Bulli paused for a moment during which Elphie held her breath. When the badger continued, his voice was surprisingly softer. "It has been a while since I ate. I've been scrounging around this pond looking for a meal, but food out here is hard to find."

"Elphie, what are you doing?" Jewels hissed under her breath. Elphie ignored her.

"Bulli," the fixie began, "Why don't you let me down and I'll open the satchel so you can have the grubs? I would be happy to share them with you."

The badger's face scrunched up as if he were thinking very hard. "I'm going to let you down," he started, "but then you have to open the satchel so I can have the grubs."

"Thank you, Mister Bulli. That would be very much appreciated."

With that, the badger untied Elphie, who went straight to the satchel and unbuckled it. Once opened, she handed the bag to the badger. Bulli emptied the satchel into his mouth and devoured the contents. His stomach quieted and his mood lifted.

"Feel better, Bulli?" Elphie asked.

"I do, thank you. So far, I'm turning over a new leaf and have given up eating meat. It's been forty days and I've only eaten the occasional grub. I will say it is tough dining outside the den." The badger paused before considering the hedgehog and flying squirrel hanging upside down. "I wasn't really going to eat you. I was just trying to scare you into giving me your lunch."

Ryart and Jewels laughed nervously. When Bulli reached for them, however, the two flinched. Instead, he untied their feet and gently let them down.

"Hey," asked Jewels, taking off her anklet and rubbing her feet. "What type of stuff do you usually eat?"

"Well, most of us badgers eat anything. I've sworn to only eat vegetables, and the occasional grub to give me a little protein punch. I do have a sweet tooth, so of course I love honey, but I haven't had any of the good stuff in forever and a day."

"Honey!" exclaimed Ryart. "Why, we just came from the willder bees' hive."

"I love me some honeycombs." Bulli's stomach erupted once more.

"Who doesn't?" agreed Ryart.

"Yes, but they have a bear problem right now," Elphie put in, picking up her discarded satchel and dusting it off. "Mortimer takes most of their honey each day."

"That's awful," said Bulli. "I'm not afraid of Ol' Mort. Us badgers aren't afraid of anything."

Jewels suddenly stood up straight, rubbing her tummy with her right hand and patting her head with her left. Elphie glanced sideways at her, recognizing her friend's thinking pose. After a few moments, Jewels spoke to the fixie in Flying Squirrel, knowing only the two of them would understand. Elphie listened, nodding her head. Finally, Elphie smiled at the Badger:

"So, Bulli," began Elphie slowly, "When you say you've given up eating meat, does that include bees and bee babies?"

"Yes, of course. I'm strictly a vegetarian now." Bulli paused, then confessed, "Just an occasional grub."

Elphie met Jewels' eyes and smiled. "That might work, then," Elphie mused.

"What might work?" inserted Ryart. "Don't leave me hanging here!"

"You'll see," Elphie assured him with a wink. "C'mon, let's go talk to the willder bees."

"But bees don't like us badgers," warned Bulli.

"That may be, but I have a plan. I'll tell you on the way. We'll have to get there by mid-afternoon. Ryart, we need you to zoom. Bulli and Jewels, try to keep up!"

◆

When Elphie, Ryart, Jewels, and Bulli arrived at the old elm tree, the swarming had subsided. The four were immediately met by Queen Zima and twenty soldier bees, an intimidating force that glared at the badger in particular.

"Your kind izn't welcome here," the queen announced to the badger in Eludian, so all would understand her.

Bulli bristled, the queen's guard readied their stingers, but Jewels and Ryart each took one of Bulli's fists.

With the tension thick in the air, Elphie spoke, "Queen Zima," Elphie said in perfect Eludian. "We come in peace."

"Not while he'z here." The queen shot a nasty look at the badger.

"Harumph," said Bulli.

"Queen Zima. Pleaze," Elphie whispered in Honeybee. "I have a propozal that might help everyone, ezpezially your hive."

The queen paused. She did not like badgers of any type; they were almost as bad as the bears who harassed her and her people. But the fairies and pixies had been friends to the willder bees for eons, since even before the Crow Wars. The queen nodded for Elphie to go on.

"If you give him honey," Elphie started in Eludian before Queen Zima cut off Elphie.

"Why would we give *him* honey?" the queen buzzed angrily.

"Because he will protect your hive from Mortimer," responded Elphie.

"How can he do that?" snapped Zima.

"Bulli here is not afraid of anything, including bears."

"But I can't truzt him. Badgerz eat beez and baby beez."

"Not this one," insisted Elphie, gesturing toward her newly made friend. "Bulli here is a vegetarian. He eats the occasional grub, but he's given up meat for forty days already."

Just then Bulli's stomach growled loudly and his mood began to shift. Jewels and Ryart tried to keep him calm, and Elphie knew she needed to seal the deal soon.

"See?" said Elphie. "He's hungry. But if you give him honey, he can help your hive."

The queen gave Elphie an unsure look, though she did signal for her guards to stand down. Her attention shifted to the badger, and her wings buzzed with more intensity as if she was judging if she could truly trust a creature like him.

A rumbling noise reverberated through the woods, making Elphie jump. She anxiously searched the nearby trees until she spotted a monstrous bear. He headed straight toward the elm tree, where the willder bees had just managed to finish cleaning up the damage from the last attack.

"The hive! The hive!" cried the guards to one another. "Protect the queen! Protect the baby beez!"

The soldiers formed a tight circle around the queen and they raced back to their home. The rest of the swarm descended on the bear, swirling viciously around his massive ears, but Mortimer ignored them, shaking off the bees effortlessly. Jewels and Ryart confirmed quietly with one another and nodded. It was time for the next step in Elphie's plan: they released their tight grip on the badger, and Bulli was off.

Before Mortimer could reach the tree, Bulli jumped between him and the hive. The bear roared in frustration, then tried to walk around the badger, but Bulli would not let him pass. He kept himself squarely between the bear and the big, beautiful elm full of honey and innocent willder bees. The badger flicked his wrists and out popped razor-sharp claws. Bulli grinned, revealing a mouthful of danger. His stomach roared, no doubt intent on the promise of honeycombs waiting for him.

Mortimer paused, took a peek at the hive, then back at Bulli. With a disinterested growl, he turned away, probably figuring he could find an easier snack somewhere else. As quickly as he'd come, the bear disappeared into the Eludian wood.

A triumphant cheer rose from the hive and the surrounding soldier bees. Elphie let out a whoop of victory, sunlight sparkling off her wings. Ryart and Jewels gave each other a high five.

Queen Zima emerged from the hive, a look of elation on her face. "We are agreed," she announced in front of the entire hive, "that Bulli the Badger will protect our hive. In exchange, we will gift him honey zo he doezn't go hungry again."

The bees buzzed their approval, including the baby bees in the distance.

The sun was setting in the west, so once the celebration got going, Elphie, Ryart, and Jewels pulled the badger aside.

"Well, Bulli," said Elphie. "It's been quite an adventure today, but I have to be home by dark. Will you be okay out here without us?"

"Will I be okay?" Bulli chuckled. "I now have a hive full of friends and I'll never go hungry again! Thank you, Elphie. You fixies sure are great at fixing problems!"

Bulli, Elphie, Ryart, and Jewels all smiled. Bulli headed back to the celebration.

"Well, good-bye my friends," Elphie said to Ryart and Jewels.

"It's not good-bye, Elphie. It's 'see you soon,'" smiled Jewels.

"Ryart, do you have one more run in you? Can you get us home before dark?"

"For you Elphie, always. Climb on." The two waved to Jewels, then zoomed home to the troupe.

◆

"How was your day, Love?" Marri Golde asked when Elphie walked in the kitchen hollow. Her mother was preparing one of Elphie's favorites: mushrooms with a pinch of pepper.

"It was good, Mama," Elphie said as she hung up her satchel.

"Hi, Nahke." Elphie held her hand to the inner wall of the kitchen hollow to feel their warmth. After a moment, a grin spread over her face when she recalled Bulli trying to rip the grubs out of her satchel earlier. No doubt that right now his tummy was very much full and happy.

"Did I hear Alice was a grump this morning?" Marri Golde inquired as she handed Elphie three acorn bowls and three spoons.

"Yes, Mama. She had a cut on her pincer."

"Did you take care of her?"

"Yes, Alice is okay now." Elphie arranged the bowls on the table, putting spoons to the right of each.

"I see. How was the rest of your day at the pond?" Marri Golde asked.

"It was great! We met a badger."

"A badger?" her mother asked with some alarm. "Aren't they dangerous?"

"He was just hungry. Bulli was actually very nice. He's now friends with the willder bees."

Marri Golde listened in admiration as Elphie shared the stories of her day. The fixie was certainly demonstrating the traits needed to lead the Emergence. By helping Alice and her friend Bulli, Elphie had shown empathy. Her daughter had listened to the titan beetle to learn what was ailing her and then had done the same with this badger. Perhaps the young fixie did have the right combination of courage, empathy, and teamwork needed to teach majesty properly to the Monarch Queen during the Emergence.

"The willder bees? My goodness, sounds like you had quite a day, Elphie."

"It was, Mama," the fixie said with a smile. "I met some grumps, but sometimes they're just misunderstood."

The Hoo Bird

Tonight was a night Elphie Askul would never forget. Winter had finally arrived, and it was time for her "First Night Out," when a young pixie or fairy was one hundred nights from their hundredth birthday and were then allowed to leave their home tree after dark. The temperature was the same year-round, but during the winter, the nights were longer. Elphie's celebration was just a few days before the winter solstice, the longest night of the year. Regardless of the season, a fairy or pixie's First Night Out was always special.

Elphie's mother still told stories about her first night out. Marri Golde and her best friends, a mud-green fairy named Eloise and a paisley pixie with long, dark curls named Peona, had spent Marri Golde's First Night Out in Dark Forest.

Elphie's mother always reminded her that this was before the Crow Wars, the woods were safer then, but still dangerous at night. "Even scarier, given none of us had earned our wings yet," Marri Golde cautioned. "I was the first of my friends to reach the milestone."

The three Wonderfolke had hitched a ride to Dark Forest with a flock of bluebirds. Marri Golde had arranged the travel by speaking to the flock in Birdling. This was a few years before the Grand Troupe Council encouraged all fairies and pixies to speak Eludian to Eludian creatures. Even today, Marri Golde still valued the old ways, so despite the Grand Troupe's strong encouragement not to speak multiple languages, the fairy had raised her daughter to use native tongues out of respect for all Eludian creatures, "When you feel comfortable, Love."

Once Marri Golde, Eloise, and Peona arrived in Dark Forest, the three spent the night playing "Fact or Fiction." The Wonderfolke each took turns asking one another questions, with the questions becoming more and more personal as the game continued. Once answered, if the questioner thought the story was true, she would respond, "Fact." If she thought the story was false, the questioner would call out, "Fiction!"

If the storyteller was caught fibbing, then the offender would have to perform an act chosen by the questioner. The acts were typically innocuous, but as the game extended into the night, the dares escalated at the same rate as the questions.

The hardest part of Fact or Fiction was that the person answering the question did not know what the dare was until after they answered. Because of this, most Wonderfolke played honestly.

But when Marri Golde was asked by Peona if the fairy thought any pixies were cute, Marri Golde's response was a resounding, "No." It was forbidden for fairies and pixies to wed; the thought of "cuteness" was a foreign concept.

However, the paisley pixie was committed to keeping her friend honest, even if the question was a little revealing. Peona and Marri Golde had been friends for decades and had formed their own friend-troupe. The pixie, however, had caught "Goldie" taking long looks at Peona's older brother, Bartholomew. The pixie wanted Marri Golde to admit her crush.

"Fiction, you old toad!" Peona screamed out triumphantly.

"What?" Marri Golde responded, acting stunned. "No, it's not. Pixies and fairies aren't supposed to wed."

"That doesn't answer the question!" Peona squealed.

"Yeah," Eloise added. "You don't have to wed a pixie to find them cute."

Marri Golde's cheeks blushed a bright blue at the thought. She knew she'd been outed by her closest friend, knowingly or not.

"Well, someone can find *anyone* cute," Marri Golde offered. "Eloise, you're as pretty as the first day of spring. And Peona, well, you're very, very nice."

"Fiction, fiction, *fiction*!" Peona argued. "You know what I meant by 'cute.' I've seen you staring at my brother. And very funny, Goldie."

"Goldie, is that true?" Eloise toyed with the fairy.

"Yes, Peona is very nice, for a pixie," replied Marri Golde coyly.

"Very funny, Goldie. You know what I mean. Do you find any pixies *cute*," Peona pushed.

"Why, I don't know . . ." delayed the fairy.

"C'mon, Goldie," urged Eloise.

Marri Golde looked at the two of them, then exploded into laughter.

"I mean, your brother is cute–for a pixie," grinned Marri Golde.

"I knew it!" exclaimed Peona. "But *gross*. He's my brother!"

"And a pixie," added Eloise. The three laughed. When the giggling subsided, Marri Golde pulled herself together.

"Don't you two ever tell anyone. Wingtip swear." With that, the two fairies and the paisley pixie all touched the tips of their wings and agreed to keep the secret amongst just the three. It was years later when Marri Golde left Homestead with Po that Eloise and Peona ever revisited Goldie's first crush.

"You don't get off that easy, Goldie," Eloise leveled after the laughing had subsided. The fairy had been caught fibbing. "You owe Peona an act."

The pixie's punishment was for Marri Golde to eat a toadstool of Eloise's choosing. Eloise selected one at random. Marri Golde did as was required, and shortly after, the three regretted it deeply. The fairy got incredibly sick. She was unable to form sentences and stared up at the stars, seemingly lost. Her two friends felt awful, but friends that they were, they delivered Goldie back home to Homestead. Hildebrund and Hildeburre grounded their daughter until the day before she earned her wings.

"On your hundredth night out," Marri Golde always ended the story, "don't eat strange mushrooms."

◆

Tonight was Elphie's First Night Out. Ryart and Jewels had helped Elphie come up with the perfect plan: the three were going to Bobo's Bog to watch fireflies. Elphie's stomach flipped with excitement when she thought about being out at night with her friends.

The evening's air was chilly, so Elphie carefully stepped into a woven, backless tunic, pulling the soft chrysalis over her hips and legs, then around her shoulders and wings. Her mother had made it for Elphie's First Night Out. The fixie admired the way the dark green color complimented her bright skin, which was so different than the other fairies and pixies.

Sometimes different is *good,* the fixie thought, though she quickly emptied her mind of the compliment. If it was good to be different, her parents would never have left Homestead. Elphie looked northwest for a moment before turning her attention back to her momentous day.

Bobo's Bog was located in the west, just north of Southern Forest. The rugged wetland was remote and difficult to get to. The bog had gray-brown hues and smelled like sulfur. It was where the delicate dancing fireflies lived. Winter was when the little insects grouped together for warmth. It was not too cold to dampen their lights, which resulted in dazzling displays of color for the friends.

The dangerous Hoo birds lived in Southern Forest, and Elphie had no interest in crossing paths with one. The Hoo bird was a creature of legend, infamous for eating anything that strayed too close to its home. Night was especially dodgy, as that's when Hoo birds went out on their nocturnal hunting sprees.

Elphie had already made a solid plan with Ryart and Jewels: by staying in the northern and eastern part of the bog, the chances of trouble were minimized. The good news was, on a pixie or fairy's First Night Out, most parents turned a blind eye to those who might be a little more adventurous. And Elphie's wingtips tingled with happiness at the idea of exploring somewhere new.

Most Eludians did not travel to Bobo's Bog, in part because it was remote, and in part because it smelled like rotten eggs. The sulfur aroma squatted over the swamp, keeping the waterway in the hands of those who valued privacy. The smell was so strong most Eludians called the place Bobo's Bottom. It was a less-than-desirable destination, making it the perfect place for a First Night Out, one that would not be disturbed by any dangerous creatures.

Elphie was meeting her friends at dusk, but her parents had asked her to stay in for dinner so they could celebrate as a troupe. To commemorate Elphie's First Night Out, Marri Golde cooked dandelions and pine nuts with a touch of sage. Her father Po did not like nuts, and he never made them for breakfast, but he did like everything his wife made for dinner. He also knew the meal was Elphie's favorite and the pixie wanted to make his only daughter happy on a night like tonight.

"You look beautiful, Love," her mother beamed when Elphie came into the dining hollow.

"Stunning," Po added with a giant grin.

"Thanks," Elphie offered, brushing off the compliments before sitting down at the table with her parents.

The young fixie devoured her food quickly and then sat impatiently as her father took forever to finish his supper. Once done, Elphie whisked away the acorn bowls and spoons before her parents had even risen from the table.

"Whoa there, Elphie," Po chuckled.

"I have to meet Ryart at dusk, Papa. I don't want to be late."

"It's winter, Love," her father responded. "The nights are longer now."

"And Ryart will wait," Marri Golde added. "I want you to please remember that there's an extra risk to you going out after dark; because you are silver, you won't be able to hide. Stick together with your friends and stay away from Southern Forest."

Elphie nodded, blowing a strand of hair out of her eyes. She was very aware of how different she was compared to everyone else who lived in Homestead. As a pixie, her father was the color of a conch shell and her mother was the lovely green of fairies. As a fixie, however, Elphie's skin was silver like a sunfish. She hated how she appeared to others. If her parents had not inter-wed, Elphie knew she would have looked like a normal Wonderfolke.

"Yes, we'll be careful," the fixie muttered. She had spent the last ninety-nine years facing life as a rare, unique creature in Eludia. Tonight, it would not be any different.

"Be home by first light," her father warned.

"Yes, Papa." Elphie tried to escape into the night, but Po coughed gently before the fixie started her descent from their home tree. Instead, the fixie returned to her parents and kissed her mother and father good night. Before she left, Elphie pressed her hands firmly against Nahke's interior and thought happy thoughts. After a moment, the fixie darted out the hollow; the nights might be longer, but the winter sun did not last long and it was setting soon. She'd have to hurry.

◆

Bobo's Bog was a wide-open wetland filled with tall grass and moss. Shrubs were scattered across the landscape. The western and southern borders of the bog were ringed by Southern Forest, a lush, evergreen wood. Elphie stood up tall on Ryart's back as they zoomed toward the stinky, secluded area. She could not wait to spot the first firefly!

Elphie and Ryart stood on the eastern shore overlooking the bog. Slowly, thousands of lightning bugs lit up the sky in blinking yellows, greens, and oranges.

Just as the light show started, an unidentified flying object swooped above them. Ryart shrieked and ducked. Elphie laughed. The aerial acrobat landed in a somersault, rolling for a few feet before popping up with a giant grin.

"Jewels! You made it!" squealed Elphie.

"Moi? But of course! I wouldn't miss it." The flying squirrel grinned at Ryart. "I scared you again, eh?"

"I wasn't scared," said the hedgehog, brushing himself off. "I was surprised."

Jewels embraced the tiny creature and stuck out her left arm for Elphie to see. "Check this out: a brand-new bracelet." Jewels showed off a glittering ring of silver. "I got it from the Ali Baba bazaar. It reminded me of you!"

"Beautiful!" exclaimed Elphie, admiring the way the moonlight hit her friend's latest piece of jewelry. Where she came from, silver things like herself were not really celebrated. Fairies and pixies were too worried about crows to draw attention to themselves. It warmed Elphie's heart to see Jewels happily flashing such a bright display. It was good to be with her real troupe again.

"By the way, love the tunic, Elphie. That green looks good on you."

"Thanks!" The fixie smiled.

The three took a seat on a patch of peat moss overlooking the bog and caught each other up on their adventures since the last time they'd met. As the lightning bugs began to paint the sky, quiet awe overtook them. Elphie thought about everything she'd experienced so far in life as she gazed up at the sky. So far, each day always ended with being home before night fell, safe in the hollow of Nahke, with her mom and dad.

But this is the start of a new set of adventures, she thought, sighing contentedly. *And very soon, I'll be able to explore day and night from up in the sky on my own wings, with my friends, and on my own time!*

Over time, the fireflies moved closer and closer to Southern Forest. The nearer they got to the wood, the more their blinking synched. Elphie craned her neck from where she sat on the edge of the bog. Why were the gorgeous little creatures fluttering away from them? She thought they had the best viewing spot, and the light show was just getting started.

"Hey, let's get closer!" Jewels urged, springing to her feet.

"Yes! Let's zoom!" agreed Ryart.

"Well, I don't know," began Elphie unsurely. "My parents said to stay away from Southern Forest . . ."

"Oh, come on, Elphie. No one is out here. It's just us and the fireflies." Jewels dismissed her, waving a paw through the air. "Ryart, what do you think?"

"I agree," Ryart stated boldly.

Elphie paused. Usually Ryart was a little more cautious, so she was surprised to find herself being the one holding back. She remembered her parents' warnings, shifting her feet anxiously. Her First Night Out could be enjoyed without going into those trees, right?

Jewels sensed her friend's hesitation, so the flying squirrel rubbed her tummy with her right hand, patted her head with her left, and then she spoke. "Hey, what if," Jewels paused. "What if we don't go into the woods? What if we just go to the edge so we can get a better look at the fireflies?"

"Well . . ." Elphie began.

"Yes! Not *in* the forest, just on the outskirts," blurted out Ryart. "That way you're technically okay. I bet the view would be amazing from over there."

Elphie hesitated, peering cautiously at her friend-troupe, thought for a moment, then stood up next to them. "Okay, I'm in!"

"Yahoo!" exclaimed the hedgehog. "Jump on my back, Elphie. We can be in the forest in no time."

"Not *in* the forest," Jewels corrected. "Just near the forest."

"Right!" The three laughed before heading south.

♦

As they neared Southern Forest, the cloud of blinking fireflies became more brilliant. The three found a gnarled, old stump that they climbed up for a better view. Elphie felt her fear begin to melt away when she caught her breath at the top of the stump. Before her, almost close enough to touch, were the inky black stretches of trees that began the Southern Forest.

But right before her eyes were countless, spinning, glorious balls of light. The fireflies embraced her and her friends, swirling around them as Elphie let out a giggle. An orchestra of crickets and bullfrogs serenaded them from below. After watching for a little while in stunned silence, Jewels turned to Elphie.

"Hey," the flying squirrel said excitedly, "do you want to practice flying some more?"

"I don't know, Jewels," said Elphie. "The last time I tried I was captured by a crow."

"That's not true!" exclaimed Ryart. "You flew at Freedo's Pond. If you hadn't, I'd still be hanging in that tree."

"Well, that is true . . ." the fixie began, unsure. Her parents would be so mad if she flew at night. But then again, they weren't here, so would they even know?

"C'mon, Elphie. It's just us out here. And we're on top of this stump, which is perfect for flying. Look, you don't have to do anything. Just watch me."

The flying squirrel stepped to the edge and opened her wings. She took a deep breath and leapt into the night. Ryart and Elphie rushed to the edge only to see their friend soaring in the moonlight.

"C'mon, Elphie! Come join me! The air is perfect," urged Jewels.

"Go for it, Elphie." Elphie looked at the hedgehog, then watched the flying squirrel as she spun through the air. Jewels seemed so free. "Go have some fun."

The fixie stepped to the edge, gathering her courage. Maybe her troupe was right. This could be the night she mastered the most necessary of skills—one hundred nights before most fairies and pixies did. With one more glance at Ryart, Elphie jumped off the stump. She was unsteady at first, but Jewels flew to her side and supported her.

"Flutter your wings, Elphie," Jewels said calmly. "Like me, look at me. Flap your wings."

Her friend demonstrated and the fixie mimicked her. Soon, Elphie was flying through the cool night air. Fireflies spun around her, twinkling in encouraging bursts of light.

"Yes! Like that!" grinned Jewels.

"That's it!" exclaimed Ryart from below. "You flying fixie, you!"

Once Elphie was comfortable, she and Jewels chased fireflies, and then each other. Ryart relaxed, rooting on his fearless friends. After some time, the three reconvened on the top of the stump, collapsing into laughter as they retold their aerial feats.

"That was great!" exclaimed Elphie.

"Yes!" added Jewels. "You're getting the hang of it!"

Suddenly, a cloud passed by the moon and darkness enveloped the friends. The lightshow stopped. The chirping went quiet.

"Hey, what happened?" asked Ryart, sitting up straight.

"They'll come back," said Jewels confidently. "Once that cloud passes."

Just then, a giant creature swooped in from the shadows. Elphie screamed and ducked. Terror froze her limbs, then she found herself able to look up. Something was pinning Jewels and Ryart down against the stump. Its sharpened talons glittered in the moonlight. Elphie leapt to her feet, facing their foe.

The cloud passed, revealing an enormous Hoo Bird. He had a large, round head with a flat, grey face and yellow eyes with dark circles around them. He was mostly silver with fine white, grey, and brown streaking. His beak was yellow and sharp. His tail tapered to a rounded end. Elphie stared in awe at the creature before her, sweat breaking out on her palms.

Ryart and Jewels tried unsuccessfully to squirm free. Before Elphie could react, the Hoo bird spoke. "Who are you?" The creature said each word slowly with a voice like liquid smoke, issuing in a smooth accent that Elphie had never heard before.

"I'm Elphie Askul," she answered steadily. "Who are you?"

"Who, me? Why, I'm Honus the Hoo bird."

Elphie examined her friends. They seemed okay but could not move under the bird's powerful clutches.

"Why do you have my friends pinned down?" asked Elphie.

"Who? The squirrel and hedgehog?" questioned Honus.

"Yes, Jewels and Ryart." The two could not even speak, so Elphie knew it was up to her to try and set them free.

"Who are they to you?" asked the Hoo Bird.

"They are my troupe," repeated Elphie.

"Who, them?" Honus shifted his weight, then rolled his eyes. He opened his broad, rounded wings and readied himself to fly. "They are my breakfast, and possibly lunch. Silver Wonderfolke don't taste good. You are free to go."

"Wait!" Elphie stepped forward, despite how tiny she felt compared to the bird's massive wingspan. "You can't take my friends."

"Who's going to stop me?" Honus retracted his wings and glared down at her.

"We will," said Elphie stubbornly. Jewels and Ryart gave her wide, frightened stares. No doubt they were wondering what exactly she, let alone they, could do to get away from such a large, deadly beast.

Elphie swallowed, then tried her best to soften her attitude as she met Honus' gaze. "Mister Hoo bird, why don't you give us a chance to go free?" she offered. Her father had often told her stories about how Hoo birds liked to play games with their food and thought it might be her best chance at freedom for her friends.

"Who, you?" Honus thought for a moment, then replied, "Perhaps I can give you a chance to go free."

"Thank you, Mister Hoo bird. That would be very much appreciated."

After a moment, Honus asked, "Who can answer a riddle?"

Ryart and Jewels looked at Elphie once more. Either they were too scared to speak or Honus' grip was so tight they could not utter a word. Elphie peered directly at the Hoo bird with as much bravery as she could muster.

"We can," Elphie said confidently, even though her stomach was doing flips inside her.

Honus thought for a moment before stepping off Jewels and Ryart. The hedgehog and the flying squirrel stumbled over to their friend and caught their breath. Elphie hugged them.

"We should escape while we can," whispered Jewels. "Ryart can zoom. Elphie, you and I can fly."

"Yes," said Ryart in a hushed tone. "There's no way he's actually going to let us go."

"No," stated Elphie. Her insides were vibrating from the adrenaline coursing through her. The fixie took a deep breath, then continued. "The Hoo bird has offered us a way out, safe and sound. If we solve the riddle, we'll be free and clear. And we'll be able to say we outwitted a Hoo bird on my First Night Out!"

Jewels and Ryart looked at each other, then reluctantly agreed. The three turned to face Honus.

The giant feathered form before them drew itself up tall. "Who am I?" Honus examined each of the three friends carefully, then continued.

"I have many hands but see with one pair of eyes. I have many ears, but only one voice. I am never alone."

The hedgehog groaned defeatedly. "We're as good as breakfast," pouted Ryart. Honus licked his beak in silent agreement. "We should never have gotten this close to Southern Forest."

"What do you mean by that?" scolded Jewels. "You were agreeing with me so easily not long ago!"

"I mean, we should never have gotten this close to Southern Forest," repeated Ryart, standing up a little straighter.

"Are you saying it's *my* fault, you undersized furball?" Jewels scoffed a little louder.

"I'm not the one who suggested we get closer," Ryart pointed out, rising to his full height. The two stared at each other until Elphie broke the icy silence.

"Hey, you two. Cut it out. It doesn't matter who said it. We've got each other's backs, which means we can make mistakes and forgive each other for them." Elphie met eyes with both of her friends. "And besides, we'll never solve this if we don't work as a team right now."

The hedgehog glanced down at the stump and scratched at the wood with his right paw. Jewels looked up at the moon, her mouth twisted in thought.

"C'mon, let's put this behind us," the flying squirrel offered quietly.

"Sorry, Jewels," Ryart finally whispered.

"This is all my fault!" Jewels exploded with sudden guilt. "I'm so sorry."

"It's not your fault, you crazy flying squirrel," sighed Ryart in earnest. "I was the one who convinced Elphie."

"No, *I* convinced Elphie," Jewels sobbed, covering her face.

"Look, you two," Elphie cut in before things could get any worse, "nobody convinced me. I'm here of my own free will." Elphie stared pointedly at her friends until they lifted their heads. "You gave your advice. I made my decision. We each agreed to get closer."

Just then, Honus shifted his feet and flapped his wings threateningly. The three friends looked at each other.

"Okay, we've got a puzzle to solve." Elphie pulled her friends in tight.

"But how can we beat the wise, old Hoo bird?" pleaded Ryart.

"Yeah," added Jewels. "How do we answer such a tough riddle?"

"Together," Elphie said firmly.

"Right on!" exclaimed Ryart.

"Jewels, can you do your problem-solving trick?" asked Elphie.

Jewels rubbed her belly and patted her head. "Nothing. I need more data."

"Okay, let's repeat the riddle again. I think it was: 'I have many hands, but see with one pair of eyes. I have many ears, but only one voice. I am never alone.'"

"That's right, Elphie," agreed Jewels.

"If we had many feet like a millipede, we could run," mumbled Ryart.

"No, Honus gave us a chance. We can do this as one," urged Elphie.

"Good, because I wouldn't want to do this alone," groaned Ryart.

"Ryart, you'll never be alone. You've got us," offered Jewels.

"Hey . . . What did you say, Jewels?" Elphie stood on her toes and fluttered her wings. The flying squirrel's words had just given her a clue.

"Ryart will never have to be alone. We're in this together." Jewels hugged the hedgehog's arm.

"That's it!" cried Elphie. "That could be the 'I am never alone' part of the riddle. Maybe it has to do with us?"

"What do you mean?" asked Ryart.

"I mean, whatever the answer is, it's never alone. Like us." Elphie's wings batted excitedly. "So maybe . . . Maybe it *is* us."

"We do have many hands," mused Jewels.

"And we do have many ears," added Elphie.

"Yes, but we have three pairs of eyes," said Ryart.

Jewels sat down, dejected.

"Maybe . . ." started Elphie. "Maybe, we're thinking about this the wrong way. Maybe it's not one pair of eyes."

"Maybe we just need to look at it together," Jewels suggested.

"That's it!" Elphie clapped her hands together. "We have many eyes, but we see whatever it is together–from the same point of view–the same eyes."

"But what about the voice part?" Ryart asked. "Do you think it's like the eyes, all seeing the same? Like all of us talking the same?"

"That could be it, Ryart," mused Elphie. "Maybe it's all of us together, just seeing and talking as one."

Suddenly, Jewels jumped up, rubbed her tummy with her right hand, and patted her head with her left. When she stopped, Jewels spoke in Flying Squirrel so only she and Elphie could understand. Elphie leapt to her feet.

"Jewels, you're right! It has many hands, but one shared vision. It has many ears, but one voice. And you can't do it alone." Elphie rushed over to the flying squirrel and embraced her. "You saved us!"

"What is it?" Ryart examined the two giggling and laughing. Before they could answer, Honus addressed them.

"Who am I?" asked Honus.

"Mister Hoo bird," Elphie held Jewels' hand and motioned for Ryart to join them. The fixie beamed with pride. "Our answer requires working together, but with one shared goal. We all have to listen, but we only have one voice. And you are never alone when you do this. Our answer is, 'teamwork.'"

"Who am I to deny your answer?" Honus paused. "You are all free to go."

"Thank you, Honus!" exclaimed the fixie.

"Thank you for not eating us," added the hedgehog.

Honus blinked, smiled, then flapped his broad, round wings and flew off into the night.

"Wow, that was close." Jewels and Ryart giggled.

"What an exciting First Night Out! I can see why my parents didn't want me to go alone. I could never have solved that by myself. In the most difficult times, you definitely find your truest friends." Elphie, Ryart, and Jewels all embraced.

Elphie suddenly looked up at the waning moon. "Oh geez, Ryart, I have to be home by first light! Can you zoom?"

"I can, Elphie. Jump on!"

"Good-bye, Jewels."

"Not good-bye, Elphie. It's, 'see you soon.'" The three embraced before leaping off the stump. Jewels waved as Ryart and Elphie zoomed.

♦

Po was awake, sitting in his snail shell in the main hollow of Nahke. He was reading the tea leaves when Elphie walked in. The young fixie rushed to her papa and hugged him tightly.

"Wow, that's quite a greeting!" The pixie hadn't had a greeting like that since Elphie was very young.

"I love you, Papa. You and Mama."

"We love you too, Elphie," Po chuckled, then pulled back and gave his daughter a serious look. "How was your First Night Out?"

"It was an adventure, Papa," the fixie replied with a smile. "We saw the fireflies and met the Hoo bird."

"The Hoo bird? He is dangerous, Elphie."

"Well, Honus was actually okay. He asked us to solve a riddle." Elphie thought about Honus. "I couldn't have done it on my own, though. The answer was teamwork."

Later that morning while Elphie was asleep in bed, Po shared with Marri Golde their daughter's latest adventure. Marri Golde knew then that Elphie now had courage, empathy, and teamwork. Their daughter would be ready for the Emergence.

The Monarch Queen

Over six hundred years ago, Marri Golde and Po had met at the Emergence. When the ceremony concluded that day, the fairy meticulously reviewed the ritual with her mother, as she always did. The youngest member of the Luna troupe wanted to understand the finer points of teaching majesty.

Marri Golde was fully aware of how important it was to welcome the Monarch Queen properly to Eludia, but that day, the young fairy was distracted by a striking pixie watching her and her mother practice. The conch-shell-pink pixie was seemingly creating reasons to work nearby. He absentmindedly collected spent chrysalis and shifted the same material to different piles, over and over again. The pixie did not approach Marri Golde immediately, but he did saunter right up to her a moon cycle later.

On the first warm spring day, Po saw the young fairy in Homestead. She was navigating the community market. The pixie angled his way directly to the fairy.

Once close, Po summoned his strength and accidentally, totally-on-purpose, bumped into the fairy. It took a moment for Marri Golde to recognize the pixie, but once she did, the fairy beamed with happiness.

"Would you like to join me on a walk through the gardens on the outskirts of Homestead?" Po said hurriedly to the fairy after they had exchanged pleasantries. He may have rushed his proposal, but the strapping pixie never took his eyes from hers.

Marri Golde was hesitant; fairies and pixies were different, and Moon and Sun forbid the two from creating troupes of their own as the strengths of fairies and pixies were meant to be opposite and separate. And yet, this pixie had caught her eye.

Po was physically fit from years of working on his troupe's farm. And yet, despite his humble beginnings, the well-built Wonderfolke carried a wonderful sense of grace about him. More so, Po was an absolute charmer when he spoke one-on-one with the fairy. Over time, the pixie's chickadee lilt would melt Marri Golde every time he sang to her.

By comparison, the young fairy was smaller, quicker, and more agile. Her lily-pad-green skin stood in stark contrast to Po's conch-shell pink. Where he was clever with his hands, she was spiritual. Marri Golde talked to the ancient animals, such as reptiles, amphibians, and insects. Her strongest sense was empathy. She certainly felt the taller pixie was interested in more than a walk.

Therefore, when Po asked her to go to the gardens, Marri Golde trusted her stomach and politely declined his offer.

The strong-minded pixie, however, would not be deterred. Po set out to befriend the fairy and worked at getting to know her. He found any excuse to visit her at her troupe's home tree.

Having earned his wings six years before Marri Golde, the adventurous pixie often traveled the deep south in pursuit of the fairy's favorite treat, honeycombs. Po bartered with the willder bees and brought home enough combs to keep Marri Golde happy and put a little happiness on his own plate.

Conveniently, the clever pixie would deliver the combs to Marri Golde's parents just before supper. As a result, her parents would almost always invite Po into their home tree for a meal. He would politely refuse at first, but upon their inevitable insistence, the young pixie would join Marri Golde's troupe for dinner.

The love-struck pixie would spend the evening listening to the stories told by Marri Golde's father, while enjoying the dinners prepared by the fairy's mother. He would even eat nuts when they were set in front of him. For the entire meal, Po never took his eyes off the beautiful Marri Golde.

After years of pursuit, Po once again asked the now-older fairy to join him on a walk. This time, Marri Golde accepted.

Their casual walks through the gardens quickly turned into long afternoons and late evenings. Being unmarried, both Marri Golde and Po lived with their familial troupes. Once their chores were completed, however, the two would meet secretly and dash off to explore the four corners of Eludia. Po and Marri Golde savored every moment together.

Po knew about the willder bees but had heard about the other parts of Eludia from his home tree. The land sounded exotic and wild, but with the crows in Dark Forest, the Hoo birds prowling Southern Forest, badgers seemingly everywhere, and the occasional bear roaming about, Eludia was unsafe to travel unescorted. Save for the adventurous First Night Out in Bobo's Bog, like Marri Golde and her friends did so many years ago, many fairies and pixies avoided the world outside Homestead all together.

Po, however, knew the land's perceived danger would provide him and Marri Golde with much-needed privacy. The brash pixie whisked the fairy off to the far reaches of Eludia, often ending up at his latest discovery, a careful clearing at the narrowest point of Deep Creek. The first time there, Po had pulled Marri Golde close and brushed the fairy's hair out of her eyes.

"I will always protect your wingtips, Mar . . ." Before he could finish, the impatient fairy leaned in and kissed her future husband. Po was stunned but thrilled. From there, their love sparked and grew exponentially, albeit secretly.

The two traveled regularly to the southern part of Eludia. They learned the dangers and how to navigate them. The pixie and fairy still lived with their parents, but the emptiness of southern Eludia soon became their refuge. What was first a game, became something more. The two soon built a life together.

As they spent more time together, their love grew as well. The two kept their feelings hidden away from family and friends, which was always the hardest part. Marri Golde and Po wanted to be properly wed, but the Old Ways prohibited the joining of fairies and pixies. They were in love. And being in love, they wanted the world to know.

Then, one afternoon just a short time past her two hundredth birthday–over one hundred years after they had met–Po decided it was time to reveal their secret. While lying in a hammock woven with dandelions, Po opened his heart to Marri Golde.

"I think we should tell our parents, Mare," Po shared. "We can't live in this fear, being ashamed of who we are and who we love. If we show them how much we care for one another, our parents will have no choice but to accept us as a couple."

"I want to believe you," Marri Golde responded, running her fingertips up and down her partner's arm. "I just don't know if they will see things the way we do. The Moon and Sun above forbid our love. More so, the Grand Troupe Council have always prohibited a love like ours."

"But why?" Po squeezed the fairy. "How can they not see how we feel about one another? Home trees are part of our troupes. Why can't fairies and pixies be a part of the same troupe? Just look at Eloise and Peona; they are in your friend-troupes and yet one is a fairy and one is a pixie. We have been patient, we have been true, and the feelings we feel have lasted for over a century. We love each other more than they could ever see."

Marri Golde wanted to believe Po, but she knew her parents felt strongly that fairies and pixies should never be mixed. That said, Marri Golde did not want to live in the shadows any longer. Sneaking outside Homestead was fun, but it was pretend. A secret relationship might survive a short while, but it was not sustainable over centuries of love. Marri Golde acquiesced.

"Okay, my love," the fairy said, squeezing her partner's arm. "If you feel we can tell them, let's do it together."

The next afternoon, Po brought his parents to the home tree of Marri Golde's familial troupe. He was confident his parents would hear their story and their love would be so apparent, there would be no option other than to accept and support their decision to marry one another. The fairy was less sure, but hopeful, and so she had convinced herself to feel the same. When she welcomed Po's parents at the hollow and brought them into her parent's home tree, the fairy was more confident in her and Po's decision. When all four parents were seated, the two took one another's hand, and began to share their story.

It could not have gone worse. The love of Marri Golde and Po was apparent, but not in the way they intended. Their parents were horrified. Both sets of parents knew the two were friends, but this?

As soon as the two joined hands and professed their affection, both sets of parents recoiled. Po's parents dropped to the ground, crying out, and beating their wings together desperately. Marri Golde's parents rushed to their daughter's side and tried to pry the young fairy away from her forbidden love. When it became apparent the two would not be separated, the wailing became screaming, and both sets of parents united in denying the relationship.

As devastating as it was, Marri Golde and Po stood firm in their convictions. As the volume increased, their grip tightened.

Finally, the crying stopped and the yelling subsided. Silence overtook the three pixies and the three fairies.

At last, Po's father spoke, "Po," his father said in a low and grumbling voice, "you must leave the Homestead. You are no longer welcome as a pixie."

"Marri Golde," the young fairy's mother said in an equally firm voice, "you must leave the Homestead. You are no longer welcome as a fairy."

Marri Golde collapsed into Po's arms. The tall pixie held his love, stared at both sets of parents, then guided the young fairy away. They had nowhere to go, so the two escaped to Milkweed Fields and settled into a fallen tree, until they found Nahke.

♦

The pain of that day had been immense, but it was long-healed before today's Emergence. Eludia was still inhabited by crows and willder bees and bear, and fairies and pixies still rarely left Homestead, but Po and Marri Golde had made a life together in Eludia.

When Marri Golde and Po celebrated their five hundred years together–an accomplishment only realized by six percent of pixies or fairies–the two did so in the privacy of their own troupe. Neither set of parents was alive to see the day, but the importance of the day–the weight of their accomplishment–was felt deeply.

To be married for five hundred years was a sign of perseverance. It was a belief in something greater than the individual and represented their undying love. The two celebrated with Nahke, their daughter, and a feast of yellow roses and violets.

Their anniversary was just a few years ago. Today, however, was the start of spring, and as such, it was a different kind of celebration. The first day of spring was the Monarch Queen's Emergence. As such, Elphie was helping her parents in Milkweed Fields. The fixie knew her friend-troupe would not be here to support her since only Wonderfolke and butterflies could participate in the Emergence. Elphie also knew the ceremony would be a long day of working alongside her father to prepare for the ceremony, then learning from her mother as Marri Golde led the ritual. The pixies would work late to collect the chrysalis. Elphie would work right alongside her father, and the ever-loyal Alice.

This was the last ceremony the fixie would not lead. Elphie's birthday was this moon cycle, but it would not fall until after the Emergence. She would be turning one hundred and able to fly soon. Next year, it would be her turn to lead the ritual.

Elphie was disappointed that she was not going to see her friends while the festivities were taking place. The fixie knew, however, that the work she would do would be important.

Just recently, the caterpillars had come from all over Eludia to prepare for the transformation of the butterflies. The fixie did not like the caterpillars. They were roly-poly lazy things that did nothing but eat her family's milkweed plants. They were not even nice to look at, with strange black, white, and yellow stripes. Elphie thought the creatures were just plain ugly.

Her parents, however, welcomed them, as her parents did with every wayward creature. The monarch caterpillars had come from all over Eludia to feast on her troupe's milkweed fields. When the caterpillars were ready to build their cocoons, they would move to somewhere safe, like the nearby woods. There, they would make their chrysalises on the trees surrounding the field.

Once created, Elphie's father and the other pixies would protect the butterflies' temporary homes by covering them in nets woven from the coconut-scented vine, cocos. The nets would protect the chrysalises from predators, such as wasps and flies. In return, her troupe would use the spent chrysalises to make clothing and other necessaries.

Pixies were stronger than fairies, so her father and the other pixies were responsible for the nets. Marri Golde would teach their queen how to fly with majesty. Today was the day.

Ever since she was a young fixie, Elphie had worked hard to learn her languages. For the Emergence, she would help her father with the nets, but Elphie looked forward to the following spring, when she would put the nets behind her and lead the Emergence. She just had to learn how to fly (*officially*, she smiled), and then she would play a vital role in one of the Wonderfolke's most beautiful ceremonies.

This morning, Elphie sat with her father in Nahke's branches and watched the fairies and pixies arrive at the bottom of Nahke's hill. It was not known when the ceremony would begin. Everyone was awaiting the first guest to reveal herself, the Monarch Queen. Marri Golde had read the tea leaves and believed the Monarch Queen's emergence was today. Po and Elphie retreated inside Nahke's hollow to get ready for the ceremony.

Marri Golde joined her husband and daughter in the dining hollow just after first light. She wore a stunning purple dress that was tight on her hips but flared out at the bottom. Pinks and deep greens wove their way through the fabric, popping on the dark purple.

"Wow, Mare," Po stammered, before kissing his wife. "You look phenomenal."

"Yes, Mama!" Elphie chimed in, grabbing her mother's hands and spinning her around. "Incredible!!"

Prior to leaving for the Emergence, Po ensured both Marri Golde and Elphie had a hearty breakfast. The pixie served mother and daughter honeycombs warmed by the first rays of sunlight, and blueberries picked just before dawn. Once fed, the three pressed their foreheads to Nahke's bark and wished the oak tree a good day. They walked down the hill, joining the other Wonderfolke.

In the morning light, Elphie could see numerous chrysalises in the woods just a short distance from the milkweed fields. The cocoons hung on branches and twigs, protected by the pixies' nets. The nets were woven of cocos, protecting the cocoons from the predators who would eat the soon-to-arrive butterflies. The monarch pupas typically took nine to fourteen days to emerge. Their arrival was imminent, but first there was work to do.

When Marri Golde arrived where the chrysalises hung pregnant in the trees, a stir washed over the crowd, followed by a heavy silence. Suddenly, the Senior Warden pushed through the crowd.

"Welcome, Marri Golde," the five-and-three-quarter inchworm fairy boomed. He wore an all-black tunic and a daffodil shaped and colored hat. The yellow popped with his toad-green hue. He made his way to Marri Golde. He acknowledged Po and said a quick hello to Elphie, before whisking the fairy away. Po winked at Elphie, then the two joined the pixies who were removing the nets from the burgeoning cocoons.

The fairies and pixies who attended the Emergence were each dressed in magnificent blues, greens, and reds. Tunics, dresses, scarves, and hats decorated the fairies. Pixies wore kilts and gloves, as they worked before and after the Emergence.

Elphie was nearly as big as a pixie, so she enjoyed working alongside her father on the nets. The last few years, Po had been teaching his daughter how to check each net to ensure their readiness. Today, Po let Elphie take the lead on the removal.

Elphie did her work, and once she was satisfied, the fixie conferred with her father. "Nice work," the pixie said, hugging his only child.

Once the nets were cleared, Elphie, Po, and all of the pixies joined the fairies and moved to a nearby large cluster of mushrooms that sat in the shade of the woods. The Grand Troupe Council sat together, with the Senior Warden positioned in the middle. The fairy representatives sat to his right and the pixie contingent to the Senior Warden's left. Po joined his daughter, held Elphie's hand, and sat on a speckled toadstool off to the side. Everyone watched Marri Golde scan the chrysalis, readying herself in preparation for the Emergence.

Marri Golde stood at the end of the woods. Her wings suddenly began to vibrate and she lifted up in the air. Wonderfolke who were not seated quickly found a mushroom cap to sit on.

"Look there, Elphie," Po whispered, pointing to a nearby chrysalis directly in the sight of his wife. The pixie could see the shuddering of a cocoon up in a nearby tree that was drawing Marri Golde's interest.

Elphie could see the muted orange and black outline of what was inside. As the fixie watched, the chrysalis shuddered and the bottom point split open, revealing the head of a butterfly. After some squirming, her antennae popped out and the glorious yellow-orange of her wings peeked through. A short rest later, the butterfly pulled herself completely free. Wet and wrinkled, the monarch butterfly held on to the chrysalis and swung her rear end out into the empty space below. Hanging upside down, she opened her wings.

Elphie oohed at her beauty, as she had many times before. It never got old; the once-ugly caterpillar was now a delicate, breathing butterfly.

The fixie noticed perhaps for the first time how beautiful her mother looked and how focused the fairy was on the ritual. Despite everything she had experienced, Marri Golde was still committed to serving the Wonderfolke.

"The Monarch Queen is the first to emerge," reminded Po, as he had for one hundred years. "She is the one your mother will teach to fly."

Marri Golde prepared to greet the newly arrived butterfly, but this time was different. Before flying up to the monarch, Marri Golde surprised Elphie. The fairy fluttered over to her husband and daughter. A murmur laced through the crowd of Wonderfolke. Elphie looked behind her to see if her mother was coming towards them for another reason.

The fairy gave her husband a kiss, then turned to her daughter. Marri Golde stared Elphie directly in the eyes and asked the fixie the most important question of her young life, "Elphie, do you know how to fly?"

"I'm not supposed to fly, Mama. I'm grounded until I'm one hundred." Elphie was close but still short of her birthday.

"Yes, I know, my love. But . . . do you know how?" The fairy gave her daughter a knowing smile.

Elphie tugged at her ear with her wingtip and shifted on the stool. The fixie looked to her father, then to her mother, then down to the earth. "Yes, Mama. I know how to fly," she confessed quietly. "I've been practicing in Far Meadow, at Freedo's Pond, and Bobo's Bog."

Her mother and father connected their eyes with one another. It was forbidden for fairies and pixies to fly without permission, but they both felt honesty was the most important aspect. And they knew a young fixie who took responsibility for their own learning had the potential to be a full-fledged member of the troupe.

It was dangerous to fly, and training was a must. However, if Elphie had survived the trials and troubles of teaching herself how to take to the air, then Marri Golde and Po knew the young fixie would be stronger for it. In the world of fairies and pixies, those who worked to teach themselves were the ones who were most successful. After all, the birds and the bees and every creature in between were not taught how to fly. They all took it upon themselves to learn the responsibility of climbing the highest rocks in Far Meadow, of fluttering over Freedo's Pond, and of exploring the night air of Bobo's Bog. Those creatures who had the courage to explore were the ones who would survive in Eludia. And those who were honest about their journey had the trust of all fairies and pixies.

Elphie was ready to earn her wings.

"Then I'm glad to share this with you," her mother smiled. "Take my hand and do exactly what I do."

"Mama, what are we doing?" Elphie whispered. She could not comprehend what was happening. The fixie's stomach did somersaults. Her parents seemed more than okay about her knowing how to fly; they seemed almost *happy* that she had.

"We are welcoming the Monarch Queen into the world. If she accepts, I will teach her how to fly with majesty while you assist. And by you assisting, this will be your first flight too."

"Officially," her father added, before kissing his daughter.

"But Mama, I don't have permission to fly," Elphie mumbled awkwardly.

"I have already cleared it with the Grand Troupe Council, my love." Marri Golde turned to the Senior Warden. The large fairy tipped his yellow hat and nodded. Excitement buzzed through the crowd. Marri Golde took a deep breath, smiled broadly, and then continued, "You are within one moon cycle of your birthday. The Grand Troupe Council has granted you permission to fly."

Elphie gasped. The crowd oohed. This was it—Elphie would no longer be grounded. The young fixie was becoming a full-fledged member of her troupe.

Elphie looked to her father, who nodded. Elphie hesitated just for a moment, took a deep breath, then decisively fluttered her wings, and rose up with her mother. Mother and daughter hovered in front of the queen of the monarchs. Marri Golde bowed her head; Elphie was a little unsteady, but she did her best to mimic her mother. The butterfly, weak from having just emerged, flapped her wings to dry them.

"Your Majesty," Marri Golde began in perfect Butterfloid, not making eye contact with the queen directly, "my daughter and I would like to teach you how to fly with majesty."

The Monarch Queen extended her antennae, putting one under Marri Golde's chin and the other under Elphie's. Gently, she lifted each of their heads.

"The queen has accepted. Now, the teaching begins." Marri Golde whispered to her daughter with joy. The fairy gazed at Elphie, reached out, and squeezed her daughter's hand. "This is it, Elphie."

The tutoring began in earnest. Marri Golde herself demonstrated how to fly with majesty for the queen. Sometimes, the fairy spoke to the butterfly in the regal, ancient tongue of Butterfloid. Other times, she communicated through tender hand gestures and smiles. Elphie drew upon everything she had learned, helping her mother where she could, particularly when the queen was unsteady on the lip of her chrysalis.

Marri Golde realized that the ceremonial aspects of the Emergence seemed almost second nature to her daughter. The years of practicing on the ground had strengthened Elphie's ritual. The challenge for the fixie was performing the ceremony while in flight. However, Marri Golde quickly recognized that her daughter was a better flyer than most Wonderfolke her age.

After a short while, the Monarch Queen was finally ready for her own flight. Marri Golde and Elphie hovered close by. As soon as the queen stepped off her chrysalis, she plummeted. Elphie's mother darted after her, grabbing the queen's back legs. The fairy beat her wings as hard as she could, but the butterfly was too big for her. The queen began to slip. A gasp went up from the Wonderfolke in attendance. Elphie's stomach boiled with insecurity.

"Papa, help her!" Elphie cried out, but her father sat on his stool.

In disbelief, the fixie turned to her mother, who was doing everything possible to keep the monarch from crashing to the earth. Elphie's insecurity metamorphosed into anger.

Then, without thinking, Elphie harnessed the anger and darted to the monarch, cradling her arms under the queen. The queen was wet and winded, but Elphie was strong enough to hold the butterfly. Marri Golde let go.

Elphie drew upon the courage she felt that first time she leapt from Condor's nest. She thought back to the empathy she had with Alice and Bulli. And the fairy drew upon the teamwork she, Ryart, and Jewels had displayed in Bobo's Bog.

"Flutter your wings, Monarch Queen," Elphie spoke in perfect Butterfloid. The queen stared at Elphie. "Like me, look at me. Flap your wings."

The monarch mimicked Elphie. The feeling was unlike anything the fixie had ever felt before. The irritation she had experienced was replaced by a feeling of accomplishment. Elphie had done something good. The fixie was teaching the queen to fly with majesty.

"Yes! Like that!" exclaimed Elphie.

Soon, the queen was able to lift herself up and out of Elphie's hold. She flew back up to her chrysalis to collect her strength. The young fixie breathed heavily but hovered in delight. Marri Golde smiled proudly.

Moments later, the Monarch Queen was able to fly on her own. It was then that Marri Golde gifted the queen a piece of her wings. The butterfly consumed the piece of wing, thus extending her life and ensuring the queen would be able to lead her followers for the upcoming year.

A short while after, the other butterflies emerged from their chrysalises and the wood was filled with bright orange and yellow insects being influenced by the queen's newfound majesty. By early afternoon, the lessons had finished and the butterflies had dispersed to spread the goodwill of the Wonderfolke.

The pixies descended upon the spent cocoons, removing the material and collecting it in giant balls of chrysalis that would be stored and processed before use. Elphie watched in disbelief as her father went with them. *Why didn't he help me and Mama?*

The thought, however, was pushed to the back of her mind when the fixie was mobbed by every fairy in Homestead. Each was grateful that Elphie had ascended to take on the ritual of the Emergence. The feeling of acceptance was something she had never experienced before.

♦

In celebration of the ceremony, when the three returned to Nahke, Po made his wife and daughter sunflower seeds dipped in honey. Elphie devoured her meal quickly. Her mother, however, took her time. Once finished, Marri Golde stood and cradled her tummy with both hands.

"My loves, I'm going to lie down for a little bit. I'm so exhausted from the day."

Elphie peered into her mother's eyes. "Mama, are you okay?" Elphie asked, trying to hide the concern in her voice.

"I'm okay, Love. Just a little tired. You did so well today. I'm so proud of you." Marri Golde bent over and kissed her seated daughter on the forehead. "I just need a little rest. I'll join you and your father in a little bit."

Po quickly stood and slipped his arm around his wife. He carefully led her to the bedroom and tucked her into a bed of moss, covering his love with lily petals for comfort. Once she was asleep, he stepped outside Nahke and into the moonlight.

Meanwhile, Elphie cleared the table and washed the acorn bowls and spoons. The fixie then joined her father in Nahke's branches. The two looked to the stars in the night sky. Finally, the fixie spoke.

"That was beautiful, Papa." Elphie started, then paused. Suddenly, she felt the anger from earlier begin to boil again. Then without thinking, Elphie blurted out a little more forcibly than she planned, "But why didn't you help me and Mama when the Monarch Queen fell?"

"It wasn't my place, Elphie. All of us have a role: pixies mind the nets; fairies teach the Monarch Queen." Po tried to stroke his daughter's hair with his wingtip, but she pulled away. Po continued, "I had to trust your mother to do her part, as she has trusted me to do mine."

"That seemed so selfish, Papa. We live here away from Homestead and away from the other fairies and pixies. It's supposed to be us: you, me, mama, and Nahke. And yet today, when we needed you most . . ." the fixie's voice trailed off. "If Mama had failed, another war with the crows could have erupted. And yet you just sat on your mushroom cap and watched. Just like us living away from Homestead. You seem to choose you and your needs over everything else."

Po listened as his daughter purged the negativity that tormented her. As hard as it had been for him and Marri Golde to be isolated from Homestead, the pixie realized then it had been infinitely harder on his first child.

"Elphie, I always put our familial troupe first," Po said with a softness in his voice. "I love you and your mother very much. I did not choose to fall in love with a fairy. We just followed the path Sun and Moon set before us."

Elphie turned away from her father.

"Elphie, my sweet love," Po continued. "I love your mother more than anyone or anything I have ever loved. My love for you is different though and infinitely greater. The love for a child is unique. You are a part of your mother and me. The best parts of me and the best parts of the one who I love most in this world. I didn't want to keep Marri Golde away from her family. But it was the Moon and Sun who gave us this gift–the gift of true love. And then with you, the gift of pure love. Your mother and I love each other, and you above all."

The fixie did not want to believe him. She had always felt so different. If anything, Elphie felt she was the *worst* parts of both of her parents.

But as she listened to her father, the fixie began to hear the truth in his voice. Maybe her differences were the good in her parents. Maybe her parent's love, despite being banished from Homestead, was good.

Elphie thought back to the all the things her father had done for her mother, like the blue-purple lobelia he was always on the lookout for, or the field of flowers he had planted specifically for his wife. Even his time on the farm was to feed and protect Elphie and her mother. Then she realized that her father had been isolated as well. Yet, he had stood by his wife, his daughter, and his home tree for over four hundred years.

Just then it dawned on Elphie. It was not her father's choice to live outside Homestead; her parents had been forced to because of their love. And their love was not a choice. It was a gift.

Then it occurred to her; if she had failed to help the Monarch Queen, she too may have been banished. The embrace by the fairies afterwards was not just for Elphie, but for her entire troupe. The fear of failure rose inside her. Panic nearly paralyzed her.

"What if the Monarch Queen had fallen, Papa?" Elphie repeated, struggling to get the words out. Without thinking, Elphie dove into her father's arms and burst into tears. Po held his daughter while she sobbed. Finally, he spoke.

"But the Monarch Queen didn't fall, Love. You had her. Your mother and I knew you were ready."

"If I had failed, we would have all been banished forever," Elphie wailed.

"No, Love," Po assured his daughter. "We knew you were ready. That's why I didn't need to help–you trusted me, you trusted your mother, and we trusted you to fulfill your role in the Emergence."

"But why did Mama pick me?" Elphie pleaded, rubbing snot from her nose with a wingtip. "I'm not a fairy. I'm too slow."

Po laughed. "You may not be the quickest fairy, Elphie, but your pixie-strength kept the Monarch Queen from crashing to the ground. And because you are part fairy, you were able to talk with the queen in her native tongue and encourage her to fly with majesty." Her father tussled his daughter's hair. "You have courage, empathy, and teamwork.

You are the perfect pick."

Elphie fluttered her wings and reluctantly smiled with pride. No one had ever told her she was perfect for anything before. "I guess I was." The fixie grinned, wiping the tears from her eyes and nestling her head into her father's shoulder.

"You are the best blend of me and your Mama," whispered Po, kissing his daughter's forehead.

The two sat in silence, listening to the songs of the crickets and bullfrogs, reflecting on the day and dreaming of what was to come.

Epilogue

After the Emergence, Marri Golde emerged from their home tree and joined Po and Elphie in Nahke's limbs. The fairy sat next to Po and held his hand.

"Are you feeling better, Mama?" Elphie asked softly.

"Yes, my love. Thank you." Marri Golde grinned gently.

The three sat in silence until the sound of bullfrogs tapered into the night. Elphie's father looked at Marri Golde and the two nodded. Still holding his wife's hand, Po put his other arm around the fairy's shoulders. They turned together and faced Elphie.

"Elphie, there is something we want to tell you," Po smiled.

"Is everything okay?" Elphie asked cautiously.

"Yes, Love. Everything is good." Marri Golde smiled at Elphie and squeezed Po's hand. "There's just something we want to tell you. It's good news . . ."

"It's great news," Po assured his daughter.

"You're both acting weird. What's going on?" Elphie straightened herself and searched both of their faces for a hint of what was to come.

"Elphie," began Marri Golde, slipping her hand out of Po's and cradling a small bump on her otherwise slim frame. "You are going to be a big sister."

"What? How?" Elphie sat back, stunned.

"Well," offered Po. "We didn't think we could, but it seems your mother is pregnant."

"A big sister?" Elphie sat for a minute, taking it all in. "I'm going to be a big sister? I'm going to have . . . I'm going to have a sibling?"

"Yes, Love," her mother offered. "Are you okay?"

"Am I okay?" Elphie asked dreamily. She paused, then her voice gathered momentum. "Yes. Yes, I'm thrilled! I just can't believe it. You're pregnant, Mama? Wow! That's great news!"

"Yes, Love. It is great news," her father laughed, looking into Elphie's earth-rich eyes. "We couldn't believe it ourselves. We are so grateful. The Weeping Tree has blessed us twice."

Elphie leapt into her parents' arms, burying her face between them.

Elphie peered into both of her parent's eyes. "A sibling . . . that's the greatest gift you could give me. I'm going to be a big sister! Wait 'til I tell Ryart and Jewels. Wow. A big sister."

"So, you're okay, Love?" Elphie's mother asked, cradling her daughter's face in her hands, stroking her hair with her wingtips.

Elphie paused, then burst into a brilliant smile. "I'm so happy, Mama. I've always wanted a kid brother or sister. Do you know which one you're having? I mean, I don't care, I'll take either, but I'd love a kid brother to take to Freedo's Pond. Or a little sister to adventure with in Far Meadow . . . or either, really, to take to the willder bees in search of honeycombs."

"We won't know until the Weeping Tree gives her blessing, Love," her father cautioned. "When we go, the three of us will travel together as a family."

"When do we leave?" asked Elphie excitedly.

"Not for a while," Po laughed. "We only found out recently."

Elphie dropped to her knees and held her mother's tiny bump. The fixie kissed her mother's tummy over and over. "It's nice to meet you, sibling," Elphie gushed. "I'm so excited to welcome you to Eludia."

"Our troupe is expanding, Elphie," smiled her father.

"Yes, we are a family, Love," whispered her mother, kissing Elphie's ear.

Elphie lifted her head, stood, and kissed both of her parents. Marri Golde and Po smiled at one another lovingly in the moonlight. The three embraced again.

In the center of Eludia, Moon smiled. She knew this was only the start of an adventure for the young fixie. What was to come was a secret shared only between Moon, her brother Sun, and the ancient Weeping Tree. Now that she had earned her wings, it was a secret soon to be discovered by Elphie Askul.

About the Author Bio

S.C. Delaney was born in Germany, raised in the US, lived in Korea, and travels to his mum's homeland of New Zealand as often as possible. Scott's debut book, *Elphie Earns Her Wings,* is inspired from a childhood where diversity was celebrated and courage, empathy, and teamwork were family gifts. Scott's message is always: Difference is strength, teamwork above all, and do good for the sake of doing good, regardless of the consequences (a message tattooed around his neck). When he is not writing, Scott adventures with his wife, Kristine, and their two cats, Walty and Jesse.

Facebook: Scott Delaney
Instagram: ArlingtonPoet
Emai: ArlingtonPoet@gmail.com
www.ArlingtonPoet.com

Reviews

"An enchanting tale where the readers are transported to the unseen magical world of fairies and pixies. Through captivating adventures, Elphie learns invaluable life lessons that resonate into our world. A delightful narrative that will inspire and uplift children and people of all ages."

—Finn O'Malley, bestselling author of the *Keeper of Elements* series and GLOWup series

"Elphie Earns Her Wings is a whimsical tale celebrating spiritedness, teamwork, and inclusion. Despite her parents' unjust banishment, young fixie Elphie forms an unbreakable, chosen family with delightful sidekicks. Together, they overcome prejudices through empathy and acceptance of diversity, connecting characters that fear would otherwise divide. In Delaney's enchanting world with real-life parallels, Elphie embraces her obligation to community, inspiring inclusivity. Delaney gracefully balances a poignant parent-child story with imaginative world-building. Readers-both young and young at heart-will cherish Elphie's ability to promote courage and celebrate uniqueness."

—Fallyn Adams, 5/6 math and science teacher, Rockland, ME

"When it comes to perseverance, spirit, and courageous fun, no one tops the fixie Elphie. Readers of any age will discover that your differences can be your ultimate strengths and that love (especially for yourself), can create beautiful magic."

—Hannah R. Lyon, bestselling fantasy author and comprehensive editor

"*A delightful fable that, through expressively colorful imagery, paints a fantastical world where all of creation is (literally) alive. Against this backdrop, it explores the learning of necessary tools for building one's own self, community, and place within the world. The main character, her family, and her companions also reinforce the importance of inclusion, and the acceptance and celebration of differences and the gifts that can be found within them. As their world grows larger and a bit more dangerous, the young adventurers come to understand that respect and teamwork build and strengthen a community. Thoroughly enjoyable!*"
　　—Dr. Nancy Tarr Hart, PhD., author, *Beyond the Veil: Unmasking the Feminine* (Volume 1); and, *Unraveling the Mystery of Mary* (Volume 2)

"*Elphie Earns Her Wings is a story of a young woman's growth and her process of discovering her own strength. S.C. Delaney creates a believable fantasy world and crafts a tale of friendship, teamwork, and self-discovery that is charming, entrancing, and inspiring.*"
　　—Carl Weaver, president, Broken Column Press; author, *Next Life in the Afternoon: A Journey Through Thailand*

"*This book is different from what I normally read, but I was quickly captivated by* Elphie Earns Her Wings: Courage, Empathy, and Teamwork. *I couldn't put it down. Elphie knew her physical difference was obvious, but watching her hidden differences of strength, wisdom, and perseverance emerge reminded me that difference is uniqueness. Elphie's story illustrates to the young and the young at heart that there is no one else who can be YOU, and that's a good thing! Wonderful, simply wonderful!! I can't wait to see what the future holds for Elphie and S.C. Delaney.*"
　　—JoAnn Harris, cofounder of A Hand Up, Huntsville, AL

"S.C. Delaney introduces us to Elphie, a charming fixie (a rare blend of fairy and pixie). This heartwarming story takes readers on an adventure, filled with valuable life lessons. Through Elphie's experiences, the author demonstrates that love transcends differences and is a powerful force to bring individuals and communities together. Thank you for the reminder that this type of magic resides in us all."

—Tina Kay, author and cohost on Dare to Rise podcast

"Elphie Earns Her Wings by S.C. Delaney is a delightfully whimsical adventure of bravery and friendship. Through kindness, teamwork, and belief in others, this little fixie learns it's okay to be different and that love is truly the universal language."

—Tiffani Freckleton, RN, bestselling author of *My NICU Story: Written with Love* and coauthor of the *Award-Winning Letters to a Future Nurse*

"I consider myself to be an aficionado of children's books, so I was thrilled to have the opportunity to review this book! My thrill quickly evolved into LOVE as I finished the first page. My love grew as I began to know the charming characters and became immersed in the world of Elphie, the fixie.

I could not put this book down, as the world that S.C. Delaney created had me captivated from start to finish.

It is a powerful storyteller who can describe something so well that the reader can see it in their mind's eye. No matter your age, I encourage you to read this powerful story of courage, empathy, and teamwork."

—Misti Mazurik, Director of Operations, RHG Media Productions

"Welcome to the fantasy land of Eludia! This wonderland has interesting characters and a gentle story. Listen carefully and you will learn life lessons about accepting differences, being brave, respect, and teamwork. It's a delightful story you will read more than once."

—Elda Robinson, international bestselling author of *One More Thing*

"Our community heavily shapes who we become. This is especially true for Elphie Askul. Although her tight-knit community is small, her world is big. It is through the unique circumstances of her birth that Elphie's character grows, developing in her a respect for and an understanding of everyone and everything in the world around her. Drawing on familial support, meaningful friendships, and wisdom imparted to her, Elphie is perfectly prepared to fulfill her purpose and earn her wings."

—Cherese A. Vines, author of *Countercharm*

"This may be a cute fictional story, but let me tell you, it is packed with life lessons, owning oneself, defying norms, and then creating a new life that takes that courageous energy to new heights The fairy and pixie in this story fell in love even though it was forbidden; love will always find a way, as is revealed here. Their daughter, Elphie-a fixie-was born from this forbidden love and is a beautiful blend of her parents' unique union. Their stories are woven into this familial network to give you a view into who they are. I found this story to be beautifully written, taking me through each phase of Elphie's life. Her natural impetus to experience the growth and strength of owning one's self, of being different with the strength to live those differences, is refreshing to read. Being different should be celebrated, not banished, as is proven by the friends she makes along the way. She brought forth her own unique blend of love, charm, strength, and above all, acceptance of everyone. This fixie embraced everyone because she embraced herself.

The life lessons in every turn of the page keeps Elphie alive and makes you want to keep turning the page to see how she survives what's next in her path to overcome, turning those obstacles into lessons of growth for all involved. Her courageous willingness to explore, her innate curiosity, and her deep desire to live on her terms against all traditions of her troupe shows her beautiful strength. Being born differently is unique, but the strength and resolve that is also born into a person who is different is stronger than anything.

My take from this beautiful story is that love prevails against all societal, so-called norms, but ultimately, you will live and love who you were meant to in the first place. Both (troupes) societies of pixies and fairies will now thrive from what she will bring to them. I enjoyed this story!"

—Steve Zeiger, international bestselling author of *My Lights: The True Story of an Authentic Life*

Elphie Earns Her Wings is the coming-of-age story of a rebelliou
half-fairy, half-pixie–fixie–who, despite her parents' exile, demon
strates courage, empathy, and teamwork to earn her wings an
become a full-fledged member of her troupe.

"A delightful narrative that will inspire and uplift children and people of all ages."

—Finn O'Malley, bestselling author of the *Keeper of Elements* series and GLOWup series

"S.C. Delaney creates a believable fantasy world and crafts a tale of friendship, teamwork, and self-discovery that is charming, entrancing, and inspiring."

—Carl Weaver, president, Broken Column Press; author, *Next Life in the Afternoon. A Journey Through Thailand*

"The author demonstrates that love transcends differences and is a powerfu force to bring individuals and communities together."

—Tina Kay, author and cohost on Dare to Rise podcast

"I could not put this book down, as the world that S.C. Delaney created had me captivated from start to finish."

—Misti Mazurik, Director of Operations, RHG Media Productions

"It's a delightful story you will read more than once."

—Elda Robinson, international bestselling author **of** *One More Thing*

Scott Delaney was born in Germany, raised in the US, lived i
Korea, and travels to his mum's homeland of New Zealand a
often as possible. Scott's debut book, *Elphie Earns Her Wing*
is inspired from a childhood where diversity was celebrate
and courage, empathy, and teamwork were family gift
Scott's message is always: Difference is strength, teamwor
above all, and do good for the sake of doing good, regardless of th
consequences (a message tattooed around his neck). When he is not writin
Scott adventures with his wife, Kristine, and their two cats, Walty and Jesse

T.J. KLAPPRODT

FROM THE SUNDERING SNOWS

AN ILBEOR STORY